The Hunter:
A Nightingale Novel

by T.M. Dawson

Dedication

For my grandfather, Glenn Riley Roye, Sr; my grandmother's, Ella and Cherril Simington; my handsome husband, Jason James Dawson; and my mom and dad for believing in me. You all are my light.

Also my editor at C&D Editing for her hard work in helping me realize my dream.

Chapter 1

He watched her, just as he had many others.

He called himself Mike, a trusting name. Those ignorant of his true intent had faith in a name like Mike. And with the handsome face he had carefully chosen by taking the soul of a victim, he could disguise his true nature.

Female victims came to him in droves. They had no idea what was going to happen to them until it was too late. This woman, Ronnie, was just like the others.

Hunching his shoulders to keep warm in the cool Scottish air, Mike salivated as he watched her walk down the sidewalk, following her from a distance, not wanting her to know he was behind her yet. It was a lesson in patience—studying prey and learning habits, like when and where they worked, slept, shopped, ate.

Mike followed Ronnie to a tattoo parlor on the Royal Mile that had a big, neon *open* sign flickering in the window. In the same window were posters, drawings of pin-up girls, and a large sign over the door that had been decorated to look as if clients were entering the gates of Hell, making it impossible to actually see inside. The sign above it read, *"Enter at Your Own Risk,"* and above that was an even larger sign that told all who came into the parlor that they would soon enter Hellish, the most popular tattoo parlor of Edinburgh, Scotland.

~~*~*

Wearing a skirt and a bodice that hugged her curvy, five-foot-four form perfectly, Nessa McRae sat at the glass reception desk, drawing in her sketchpad. She ran a hand through her black hair with its red streaks and looked around the tattoo parlor.

Hellish was located on the Royal Mile. Tattoo art sat in frames along the walls, along with drawings of women, colorful birds, and anchors with the name "*Sailor Jerry*" printed on them. Of course, there was also art from Nessa and Billy, her father and Hellish's owner.

The parlor had a floral smell to it and was arranged with comfortable chairs in the lobby, a small, see-through coffee table shaped like a coffin that held their snake Pip, and the glass reception desk that held a display of shirts, tattoo ointments, soaps, and a variety of studs and rings for piercings next to a door that read "*Employees Only*."

As she started watching her lazy snake, Nessa looked up at hearing the bell ring above the door and smiled at the woman who entered.

The woman, Ronnie, sat down just as Nessa's dad and Hellish's owner, Billy, walked out of his office with their guest artist, Jimbo, an asshole from somewhere in the Southwest, United States. He was currently under suspicion for trading sexual favors with Ronnie for tattoos. They weren't really sure, though, and Nessa's dad had been trying to catch Jimbo in the act for a while now.

"She cause any problems?" Billy asked after Jimbo and Ronnie went into the back room.

Her dad was a burly, tall man, who stood over many people at six feet and was intimidating. He always had a stern look on his handsome face, and he had a scar going from his left eye to his jaw, which he had gotten when he had been in the military. His whole muscular body held an aura of *don't fuck with me*.

"No, but I'm sure she's not here just for her tattoo coloring."

Billy nodded. "I'll keep popping in to check out his work from time to time. Maybe today will be the day that I catch him."

Nessa nodded then grabbed her sketchpad to finish something she had been working on all day.

Billy leaned over to take a peek, but Nessa tilted the sketchpad toward her. "It's not finished yet."

"What is it supposed to be?"

"Well, it's going to be a portrait of two demons in battle against each other. No faces yet, and their wings haven't become clear to me. It would make for a very nice tattoo."

Billy smoothed out Nessa's hair then kissed the top of her head. "You'll figure it out; you're a natural artist. Whatever you draw always comes to life." He smiled as he pushed back a strand of her red and black hair from her face. "Whoever ends up wearing it will be lucky to have your art."

She gave him a skeptical look.

"It's true."

She smiled. "Not as good as you, Dad."

He nodded. "True." Then he patted her on the shoulder and went into the back room.

~~*~*

Mike watched as the door to Hellish opened. *About damn time.* But the woman who walked out wasn't Ronnie. She had long, black and bloodred hair past her shoulders and wore a bodice, leggings, and a short skirt that complemented her hair, if he said so himself.

This woman was someone who treaded that thin line humans tended to cross. Fat, thin, beautiful, or ugly—nothing seemed to matter to her.

As the woman walked down the street, he followed her, completely intrigued. She smelled good, too.

~~*~*

Nessa walked into the Chinese restaurant that Billy and she loved to order from on long work nights. It had been there since she had been a scrawny child, only allowed to play in Hellish's upstairs apartment while her father worked.

The well-lit restaurant was decorated with Chinese art and smelled of rice, noodles, chicken, and soy sauce that drove in hungry customers. Their chairs were comfortably soft for those who enjoyed the buffet in the banquet room, and the tables held more Chinese art that greeted the customer when they sat down. It was truly a comforting place, with just as comforting music.

A few men in the corner, whom she knew to be the restaurant's regulars, stared at her as she came up to the counter. Nessa brushed her hair from her face and smiled at them. They shot her toothless grins of their own.

Nessa then smiled at the cashier and ordered as she reached into the pocket of her dress for her money clip when someone suddenly pushed her into the counter from behind. She glared back at the person, seeing a man wearing blue, mechanic's coveralls look at her apologetically.

His face was tan and unshaven, with high cheekbones. He had short, reddish hair and the strangest color eyes. They were reddish-yellow and had to be contacts. He was handsome, though, despite being a little greasy from work.

"I'm sorry," he said in a deep voice that made the hair on the back of her neck stand on end. "I didn't mean to do that."

"It's all right." Nessa grinned while looking him up and down.

"Just got done working on my niece's car," he told her with a giant smile as he brushed at his coveralls.

To Mike, she looked even better up close, with her creamy, unblemished skin; beautiful blue eyes; and red, full lips. Her breasts weren't half bad either. She was perfect. Exactly what he had been looking for in a mate.

Nessa paid for her order then smiled at him again, thinking, *A yummy mechanic. Not too bad.*

She dug a card out of her pocket then handed it to him. "Come by sometime. Maybe I can find you a tattoo that you will love"—Nessa fingered his name tag—"Mike."

"I would like that." Mike looked at the card. "Nessa. Pretty name for a beautiful woman."

Nessa smiled as she grabbed her bags then left the restaurant.

"Can I help you, sir?" the cashier asked.

Mike ignored him, following Nessa back to Hellish.

~~*~*

Nessa ate her fried rice as she stared out the window of Hellish's small breakroom, looking across the hall at the man sitting in her dad's chair. His name was Ailes, a six-foot tall, tanned, tattooed, muscular man. His face was elongated, with a broad forehead and angular cheekbones. He sat there with his eyes closed, his dark eyebrows frowning slightly, while her dad worked on his muscular chest.

Nessa ate another spoonful of rice and looked at the sketch she had been working on. It irritated her that she wasn't coming up with anything else to put into the drawing.

She ate more rice, looked back at Ailes, and froze.

He was staring right back at her.

She turned her attention back to her rice, trying to forget those eyes and the cocky smile that he was currently aiming her way. Ailes rarely smiled when he came into the parlor.

"Dad, it's time for your lunch break," she called to him, shifting on her feet and looking at the skull drawing on her dad's wall. Really, she was looking at anything besides the sinfully handsome man in her dad's chair.

"I'll take my break when I'm done," Billy responded as he continued to work.

If he didn't eat soon, his blood sugar would drop.

Nessa grabbed her sketchpad and left the room, making her way to the front, where she sat down at the reception desk and turned to a blank page to begin another drawing. When she looked up again, she found Ailes staring at her again.

She ground her teeth, tapping her fingers on the glass desk as she tried to calm the nerves that she suddenly felt. Why did he do that to her?

"Can I help you?"

Without a word, Ailes pulled out his wallet, threw down a wad of bills, and then left the parlor.

Nessa breathed out a sigh of relief.

~~*~*

Billy put his arm around Nessa's shoulders as they crossed the street, heading straight toward Mike, who was well-hidden behind a dumpster. He watched as they passed him on their way to the car that they shared.

Once they rounded the corner and were out of sight, Mike crossed the street toward Hellish. He knew the layout of the building; where he could enter without setting off the alarm.

Mike walked to the back of Hellish, pulled down the fire escape ladder, and then climbed up to the apartment. He hoped that fool, Jimbo, had left the window unlocked.

Excitement burned within him as he entered the apartment. Mike loved the hunt. It coursed through his blood. Learning about his prey gave him a sense of ecstasy, almost like the effects a good drug gave paired with alcohol.

Mike walked out of one room, into the small living room, and to the front door, where there was a stairwell that led to Hellish's back office.

In the far corner of the room sat a desk and computer. Besides that, there was a filling cabinet. Mike crossed the room to the cabinet and growled. Locked. He ended up having to break it open, revealing hanging folders. There were tax papers, business receipts, and finally the folders on each employee. Mike grabbed Nessa's file, jotting down her address and birthdate. It was coming up soon. Maybe he would give her a present.

Chapter 2

The next afternoon, Nessa walked into work to find Billy talking to another guest artist. She walked over to them, clocked herself in, and then put her things under the reception desk.

Billy and the guest artist came over to her.

"This is my daughter, Nessa." Billy looked at Nessa. "Nessa, this is Samuel. He is going to be our guest artist until next year." Billy smiled at them both then turned toward the door as it chimed. He nodded at Ailes as he walked through the door before continuing, "Jimbo's time has come to an end. If he comes in, call the coppers."

Samuel looked at Nessa and smiled. He was tall, muscular, and had an angular, handsome face with perfect teeth. His neck was covered in tattoos that disappeared under his shirt and reappeared down his arms. He was perfect for Hellish and pretty man meat for the girls to ogle.

Nessa smiled back then gave him a tour of the parlor, finally ending in the apartment where she handed him the keys. "Have a nice stay and welcome to Hellish. I can't wait to work with you."

Samuel thanked her then went about getting his things unpacked

As Nessa walked down the stairs, she felt the hairs on the back of her neck stand on end. She turned and looked out the window that faced the alley, seeing Mike standing there, staring at her. She smiled and met him by the parlor's back door.

"Enjoying the sights?" she asked.

He just continued to stare, beginning to creep her out.

"Hello?"

Mike snapped his gaze to hers and, for a second, she thought his eyes turned from green to black.

"I am sorry, pretty Nessa. I was lost in thought," he said. "I was passing through and wanted a good look at the parlor and the apartment above. I see you have a new tenant."

Nessa looked over at Samuel as he carried things up to the apartment from his truck. "Aye, he's a new artist for the year. Our last artist lost his job with us. Broke some rules."

Mike smiled. "Ah, Daddy has rules, does he? Well, you know rules are made to be broken."

She nodded. "Yeah, well, I have a client. I hope to see you soon for a tattoo." She quickly walked away and into the parlor. When she closed the door, she was able to breathe normally.

Come to think of it, she had never told Mike that her dad owned the parlor, but of course that was public knowledge, as her dad was always in magazines or the local newspaper around Edinburgh for his outstanding artwork.

Mike seemed different from the night when she had first met him. Maybe it was just nerves, since she was meeting a new client.

Dad came out from the back and smiled at her. "You have a new client in your workroom. Seems like you're in for a handful today, my sweet."

Nessa walked to her workspace and peered in through the window. She rolled her eyes.

Great. Ronnie for another tattoo.

What was she going to tell her about Jimbo? Everyone knew that he and Ronnie were an item.

Nessa smiled and walked into the room, closing the door behind her. "Hello, Ronnie. What is it going to be today?"

~~*~*

"Do you want to add this design to the one we finished yesterday or is this going somewhere else?" Billy asked Ailes as he looked at the picture he had given him.

"I want it on my chest," Ailes answered, patting to the left of his breastbone.

Billy nodded. "I'll have Nessa set you up an appointment for tomorrow night to give me time to come up with a design."

"No, I want it done tonight," Ailes said, pulling out his wallet. Taking out some cash, he tried to hand it to Billy.

"No, keep it." Billy stood. "If you want it done tonight, I can fit you in. Just remember that I don't do this for just anyone."

Ailes put the money away as Billy left the room to go draw up a design and a stencil.

Ailes knew Billy didn't just do spur-of-the-moment tattoos, but this sigil was important. He needed it on his skin like a kid needed a sticker.

Not one to sit still, he stood and walked back up to the front.

Billy nodded at him as he passed the back office, and then Nessa looked at him as he passed the front desk to look at the flash art on the walls.

"Bastard," Nessa mumbled under her breath.

Ailes looked at her, and Nessa quickly looked back down at her sketchpad. He almost walked away, ready to forget what Nessa had said, but he was riled up today. A hunt had gone bad, and he wasn't in the mood to deal with assholes.

Ailes wasn't upset with the word—hell, he *was* a bastard—but he wanted to see her squirm.

Ailes leaned over toward Nessa, and when she didn't back away from him, he got closer. Finally, she reacted just as he knew she would—by slamming her sketchpad on the desk and standing.

"Say that again," he dared.

Nessa didn't say anything, knowing it would be better if she just apologized then went back to her drawing. But this was a matter of pride, and it was evident on her face

"If that's what you want, *bastard*." Nessa narrowed her eyes at him.

"For someone so muscular, I bet you have a small penis."

Ailes laughed then closed the distance between them until his lips were next to her ear. "Why don't you feel it for yourself? You know you want to," he whispered softly then took her earlobe into his mouth and nibbled on it.

Nessa froze, her body quickly betraying her.

She extracted herself from him and, before he could dodge it, slapped him hard. The sound reverberated around the parlor, bringing Billy and Samuel out from their rooms.

Billy stared at them, seeing Ailes was standing too close to his daughter. So close that he could have kissed Nessa. The left side of his face was red and had the faint imprint of Nessa's hand, yet Ailes looked relaxed.

Billy balled his hands into fists. He wasn't taking any shit in his tattoo parlor.

Ailes smiled, walked over to Billy, patted his shoulder, and then made his way back into the man's workroom.

~~*~*

Nessa's face burned as she stared at Ailes, her hand stinging and her body tingling.

She had stood up straight and had refused to back down from the handsome man. There had been no obstacles keeping Ailes from hitting her back because, during the altercation, the two had moved away from the desk.

Then Ailes had smiled at her.

Billy gave her a look and gestured with his head that we wanted to talk to her outside.

Huffing, she stomped her way out the door.

"What in the hell happened in there?" Billy demanded once the door closed behind them.

"He wouldn't back off, so I slapped him," Nessa answered, leaving out what Ailes had whispered to her and the fact that he had nibbled on her ear.

Billy shook his head. "You have to stop doing this. That's the second time this month. First with Jimbo and now with Ailes."

"Jimbo was a perverted ass. He deserved that boot."

"And Ailes? Did he really deserve a slap?"

"Ailes is an ass, too. And if you had been there, you would have punched him for what he said to me."

Billy sighed. "Nessa, my love, I am your father, and I know you better than anyone. You had to have said something to warrant Ailes' anger."

"So, you don't believe me?" Nessa scoffed, her face hot as she crossed her arms.

"It's not a matter of me believing you. My love, you don't bite the hands that feed you, no matter what they do." Billy pulled her into a hug and kissed the top of her head. "I want you to go home and rest. And before you say anything, this is not a punishment."

~~*~*

Nessa leaned against the kitchen counter while the water for her tea heated in the kettle. When it whistled, it broke her away from the day's thoughts. She really shouldn't have been thinking of Ailes anyway, but him using his mouth on her ear like he had had her touching it, shivering.

She picked up the tea kettle and poured the water over the green tea bag in her mug.

"Stupid," she berated herself when she took a sip and burned her tongue. "Dammit, get it together."

She slammed her cup on the counter and stared at the liquid sloshing inside. What could Ailes possibly have that interested her? How about a nice ass and tight body that she would like to see fully naked?

She closed her eyes and pressed the heels of her hands into them. Then she walked to the sink and poured the tea out. She wouldn't have enjoyed it anyway.

"Such a waste," she commented, heading toward the bathroom,

stripping her clothes off along the way.

~~*~*

Still reeling over the events from earlier, Nessa rolled her eyes when her cell phone rang. All she wanted was to be left alone.

"Hello?" she answered gruffly.

"Hey, Nessa, this is Mike. I was wondering if you were free tonight for an appointment?"

Nessa looked at the clock then rubbed her face. "No, but I am free tomorrow night."

Mike clenched his fist. *Damn that half-breed.*

"All right, tomorrow then."

"See you then," Nessa told him then hung up.

Chapter 3

Mike entered the parlor the next night, looking at all the art along the walls and smelling the room's floral scent as he made his way toward the reception desk. The man he had seen moving in yesterday sat before him, reading a romance novel.

Mike cleared his throat, and the man looked up from the book.

"Can I help you?" he asked.

"I'm looking for Nessa. I have an appointment," Mike answered.

The man frowned. "I wasn't aware she had an appointment this late." He turned toward the computer.

"He's with me, Samuel," Nessa called as she walked out of her workroom and smiled at Mike.

Mike wore a button-down, plaid shirt and blue jeans that hung on his hips perfectly. His face was clean shaven, and his hair was combed to the side. There was a hint of what Nessa thought might be cologne permeating the air around him.

Samuel nodded then went back to his novel.

"This way," Nessa said, opening the door from the lobby to the back rooms.

~~*~*

Normally, Ailes wouldn't care who walked through Hellish's halls, but something was off about the man following Nessa. His smell permeated the air—the smell of death.

Ailes narrowed his eyes and looked closer. The man's face shifted slightly. That was when he knew.

Ailes cursed under his breath.

~~*~*

Nessa walked into her workroom and motioned for Mike to sit in the chair. She then walked over to her cabinet and pulled out the sketchpad that she always kept there.

"Please tell me you know what you want. Because, if you don't, then I'm afraid I will have to reschedule you for another night," Nessa informed him, still keyed up from her spat with Ailes the day before.

Mike chuckled. *Spunky.* He liked his human women that way. They put up more of a fight.

"Yes, I know what I want," Mike answered. However, the way he said it made Nessa feel like they weren't talking about a tattoo anymore. Still, she let it go.

"What did you choose?"

Mike smiled. "How about a crow?"

Nessa smiled at Mike, touching his arm. "Why not a pin-up? You look like a man who appreciates a good woman."

Mike laughed. "You have no idea."

Nessa turned away to pick up her sketchpad. "Where would you like your crow?"

"How about my face?" Mike stood and pressed his body against her back, relishing the feel of her butt tight against the hardness between his legs.

Nessa froze. This wasn't the first time a man had gotten fresh with her. It happened occasionally. Hell, Ailes had just tried it last night. Nevertheless, Nessa was confused by her reaction to the sudden presence. It thrilled yet alarmed her at the same time.

The smell of sulfur permeated the air around Mike as his body melded with hers.

"Mike, please move."

Mike sniffed her hair. "You're very beautiful," he whispered.

"Maybe we can come to an arrangement."

Nessa closed her eyes tightly and repeated, "Mike, please move."

He laughed.

Nessa pushed him back and swung her arm out, slamming her fist into his face over and over again until she felt her wrist and arm snap. She screamed as she cradled it against her chest.

"You bitch!" Mike screamed, punching her in her face.

She flew into the cabinet then fell to the floor. She felt her arm snap again and screamed as the pain from her arm, face, and body blinded her. Then she grabbed a hold of the counter and pulled herself to her feet.

She stared at Mike as he thrashed around the room, his face covered in bright red blood. Had she hit him that hard?

Nessa frowned and brought her hand up, staring at the blood and her tattoo gun. Just what had she done? It had to be ink from her gun, right? It just had to be. She hadn't even known she had grabbed the tattoo gun.

Nessa looked back at Mike, seeing his face was riddled with deep cuts. It didn't look the same anymore.

Instead of the handsome face, there was a skull with horns; high, red cheekbones; and eyes that were sunken in. Blood poured from one of those eyes, mixing with the blood from the wounds on his face.

Nessa closed her eyes then reopened them, hoping what she had seen would have just been a figment of her shocked mind. It must have been because it was back to the torn flesh.

Billy, Ailes, and Samuel suddenly burst into the room, having heard her and Mike's screams and the commotion coming from her room.

Ailes looked at Mike then at Nessa, at the blood on her hand, and the tattoo gun she held.

His face in shreds, Mike tried desperately to keep his disguise intact as he hissed, looking straight at Ailes.

Ailes couldn't help wondering, *Why do I always have to be at the wrong place at the wrong time? Even worse, Why do I have to be the one who runs into a demon. Every. Single. Time?*

Mike hissed again then bum-rushed Ailes.

"Dammit," Ailes whispered as Mike slammed into him.

They crashed into the hallway, and then Mike stood, grabbing Ailes' long, raven ponytail and using it to drag him into the lobby, where he threw him into the reception desk.

Ailes pulled himself up, knocking over the computer, right before Mike tackled him into the chairs. Then they both stood, and Ailes managed to grab Mike's shirt, dragging him toward the exit. Before he could get Mike out the door, though, the demon grabbed Ailes' pant leg and used his body to throw him and Ailes through the glass door, crashing them out onto the sidewalk.

Passersby screamed and scrambled out of the way as both men rolled on the sidewalk, punching each other.

Nessa ran out of the parlor, still not sure what she had done to Mike, and watched as the two men fought. Something was off.

She winced as a sharp, hot pain pierced through her arm and wrist as she watched Ailes throw another punch, his fist connecting with Mike's face, which shifted back to a skull with sunken eyes.

Nessa shut her eyes and shook her head. When she reopened them, she saw that Ailes and Mike had rolled into the street.

Ailes pushed away from Mike, and then they both stared at each other.

"You are a fool to show your face around here!" Ailes yelled. "These aren't your hunting grounds."

Mike laughed. "Who are you to tell me where I can't hunt, half-breed?" He licked his lips. "Devouring you will be so sweet."

A horn blared in the distance, and Nessa turned to the source of the sound, watching as a car careened toward Ailes and Mike.

"Ailes!" Nessa screamed as she bolted toward the men, who had also turned toward the sound.

Ailes then turned to find Nessa coming right for him, colliding into him.

He held her tightly as he jumped them out of the car's way.

Mike screamed and tried to lunge after the couple. However, the car had blared its horn too little too late for him in his injured state, and Mike crashed through the windshield.

The driver slammed on the brakes, sending Mike flying away from the windshield and onto the street.

Ailes and Nessa stood and watched as the driver walked over to where Mike had landed, but the demon was gone. He then looked at Ailes and Nessa as he took out his cell phone.

~~*~*

Mike pulled the last of the glass from his arm as he stared out from the alley that he was hiding in. *Damn filthy humans*, he thought as the police arrested the half-breed and talked to Nessa.

He watched as Billy walked Nessa back into the tattoo parlor and as the police drove away with Ailes in the back of their car.

Mike pulled another glass shard from his torn face then brought his hand down and stared at the blood on his fingers. Mike laughed as he licked it off. Oh yes, he really loved feisty women.

Chapter 4

After calling to make sure that Nessa and her father were all right, Ailes then made a call to Brylan, a detective and childhood friend whom he told to meet him at Ailes' apartment.

He had been released from police custody when Billy had called ahead to tell them that Ailes had helped take out the riffraff from his shop, telling the officer that Ailes had been protecting his daughter and that the fight had escalated.

"What's up?" Brylan asked, meeting Ailes outside of his apartment building an hour later.

"Not here. Let's go inside for a drink."

Brylan followed Ailes into the apartment and watched him check the place over before he poured them both a glass of whiskey then handed one to Brylan.

"The hard stuff? I guess something happened tonight that has you on edge."

Ailes took a long draw off his drink. "I saw a shadow demon tonight."

"Where?" Brylan asked, staring into his glass.

"Hellish, the tattoo parlor. He attacked a woman there. Billy's daughter, Nessa McRae."

"Shit." Brylan took a drink of his whiskey then motioned to the bottle. "Give me the whole damn bottle. I have a feeling this will take a while."

Ailes stared at the whiskey in his cup. "He knows who I am."

"Dammit, Ailes. How did he find out?"

Ailes took another swallow of his whiskey. "I attacked him after he attacked Nessa."

"For fuck's sake, Ailes, you know how dangerous shadow demons can be. Even you cannot take on a full shadow demon," Brylan chastised. "What were you thinking?"

Thinking with my cock.

Ailes stared at the detective. "I didn't know he was a shadow demon when we fought." He took another drink. "He won't be coming after me, anyway, not after what Nessa did to his face."

Brylan's eyes went wide. "She injured a shadow demon?"

Ailes nodded. "Not just injured. Tore the shit out of his face." He traced own his own face from eye to chin. "He won't likely have an eye anymore. She did a number on him."

"With what? How?"

"Tattoo gun."

"Fucking hell. It's bad enough you fought him, but now a human manages to injure him with a fucking tattoo gun?" Brylan shook his head. "You know that, if he has a family, they will likely be looking for her. I will have to alert the Nightingales of this."

The Nightingales were a secret organization that protected the paranormal world and its inhabitants. They normally didn't deal with humans, unless those humans were connected to the supernatural world somehow

Ailes shook his head. "I will help her. Keep her safe." He took another drink. "I owe her that much since I made it worse by associating myself with her, and they will attack her because of me, not just because she managed to injure the demon."

Brylan sighed. "Fine, but you have to do something quickly. I can't keep the Nightingales away from this. They may already know about the attack and will likely be watching Nessa. Can you tell me the shadow demon's name?"

Ailes grabbed a card from his wallet and wrote it down before handing it to him. "I don't know if he will be in the Nightingales' system."

Brylan pocketed the card. "If he is, I will know. I will be in touch." He walked toward the door. "And Ailes?"

Ailes looked at him.

"Keep your dick out of this. We don't need him thinking you're competition. You know how shadow demons get when there is something they want."

"I won't," Ailes said. "She's not my type, anyway." *Liar!*

Brylan nodded. And with that, he left the apartment.

~~*~*

An hour later, Ailes stepped out of the shower and looked at the woman sitting naked on his bed.

"Come here, sweet thang," she crooned.

"No. You need to leave," Ailes told her.

The woman whimpered then pulled him to her when he walked by the bed, hurriedly putting him in her mouth.

Ailes growled and pushed her away. "I said no, Ronnie. Now leave."

Ailes had been craving a warm body, someone to fill his bed, and she was the only one who could take his inhuman strength enough to sate him. She was also the only woman who didn't try to trap him into a relationship and did as she was told. Sometimes.

Ronnie licked her lips, disappointed. "Fine." She stood and pulled on her dress. "If you need anything else, just call." She walked out of the room, swinging her hips, trying to entice the man whom she had just had sex with for the past hour.

Ailes growled as he watched her walk down the hall. Instead of imagining *her* naked, he was imagining a certain black-haired beauty from a certain tattoo parlor.

Ailes walked into the hallway, grabbed Ronnie, and then pushed her up against the wall. The woman laughed, wrapping her legs around his hips as he entered her.

~~*~*

Nessa slammed her ink cupboard shut as she walked around her workroom and cleaned up the mess that bastard had left behind. He had nearly destroyed *everything*.

She looked at the tattoo gun that had saved her life. It was bloody, and the gun was broken. How in the world was Mike still alive? She had stabbed him in the face and torn up his eye. He should have been dead, but the man had still been alive, even after Ailes had gotten involved.

Nessa picked up the tattoo gun and hurled it across the room, narrowly missing her dad as he came into the room with Samuel close on his heels.

"*What the hell is wrong with you?*" Billy boomed. "That could have hurt us!"

"Whatever. It wouldn't be the first time the damned thing was used to hurt someone," Nessa said.

Samuel looked at the tattoo gun now lying next to the workroom door. He pulled some latex gloves out of the box on the wall, pulled them on, and then picked it up. "I am going to see if maybe any of this can be salvaged. It won't be able to be used for any more work, but hey, at least you will have a souvenir."

Billy looked at the man. "That isn't helping. Just get rid of the damn thing."

When Samuel left, Billy brought his attention back to Nessa. "You will be taking two days off, and I will hear no argument from you."

Nessa crossed her arms. "Why? So that bastard can come finish the job?"

"No, so you can blow off your anger." Billy pulled her into a tight hug. "You are scared and the adrenaline is still fresh. I know it's hard, but I really need you to stay away from the business. I also need you to

21

go to the hospital. That arm doesn't look good."

Nessa pulled away. "You think it's broken?" She stared at her arm, which was now a deep shade of purple. She tried to flex her hand and found that she couldn't do so. She thought back to the fight and winced. She had felt it snap when she had punched Mike. Why had that broken her wrist and arm?

"I don't think. I know." Billy pushed a strand of hair from her face. "Nessa, what happened tonight was hell, not just for you but for me as well. When that man attacked you … I thought for sure I would lose you. But then Ailes got involved."

Nessa shook her head, grabbed her bag from the cupboard, and then slammed it shut. "I will go to the hospital. And Ailes was only protecting himself." She walked out of the workroom then out of the parlor.

Billy shook his head and looked around the room at the mess and blood left behind. He sighed then began to run the numbers through his head. It was going to cost him big time to replace the damn glass case and window as was, and now he would have to get a cleaning crew to come in. He just wished he had watched Mike more carefully.

Chapter 5

Two days of nothing but watching T.V. and eating spoonful after spoonful of ice cream with her good arm. The visit to the hospital had revealed that her arm was, in fact, broken, but no other injuries. Despite that, there had been no word from her dad about coming back to work.

Nessa drank a bit of her green tea while staring at her phone, willing it to ring so she could go back to work. Then she put her head down on the table, and when her phone didn't magically ring at her thoughts, she stood. If her dad wasn't going to call her to come in, she was going to work anyway. She was a grown woman, dammit.

Nessa walked out of her apartment and toward Hellish.

A few blocks away from her apartment, she rounded the corner and stepped onto the Royal Mile as she kept her good hand warm in her jacket.

A wisp of a shadow flitted at the corner of her eye, and Nessa turned to find no one behind her but tourists down the street and the residents of the city. Must have been a cat. She continued on her way, passing an alley.

Nessa then jumped as the same shadow appeared and disappeared into the alley. She ran the rest of the way to the parlor, only stopping and turning back around when she had made it to the gated door. No one was there but an elderly couple taking pictures of each other.

Nessa continued to look around and saw Ailes walking down the street, away from Hellish. She clenched her jaw and walked into the parlor, startling Samuel, who had been reclining back in the chair and had to catch himself with a hand on the desk.

Once in the back office, Nessa opened the filing cabinet and found Ailes' file. She typed his address into her phone then closed the cabinet and pretended to look for her sketchpad when her dad came into the room.

Billy looked at Nessa suspiciously. "Why are you here, baby doll?"

"I was going to work, but something came up suddenly," Ness said as she walked out of the room.

"I told you to take time off. I will keep an eye out for your sketchpad." Billy nodded. "But take the car."

"Way ahead of you."

Nessa walked to the car in the parking lot behind Hellish and pulled her phone from her pocket. She set Ailes' address into the GPS. Time to kick creepy stalker's ass.

~~*~*

Ailes flexed his arm and brought up the dumbbell, his muscles bunching and relaxing as he pumped his arm. The kitten at his feet bit his toes and ankles in play, and Ailes laughed as he set down the dumbbells and picked her up to scratch her behind the ears.

When a knock sounded at the door, he stood and answered it.

Ailes barely dodged the fist that nearly got him in the face. He set the kitten down and stared at the woman in front of him.

"What are you doing here, Nessa?" he asked, raising his eyebrows mockingly at the arm in a sling that he had seen earlier.

"You know why I'm here, asshat."

Ailes raised his eyebrows. "Do I?"

"Don't play dumb with me. You've been stalking me since I left my apartment," Nessa explained as she walked into the apartment.

Man, she was out of her mind.

He laughed and wiped his face. "And, why do you think I would follow you? What makes you so special? Besides, you are the one following me now. You having stalker tendencies? Oh, and make yourself at home?" he retorted as she started going through his things.

"I don't know. Maybe you're attracted to me," Nessa said, peeking up from going through his mail.

Ailes laughed. "Yeah, I do have an attraction, a strong one." He sauntered over to her and towered over her, bringing his face barely inches from hers.

Nessa frowned and opened her mouth to fire something back at him but was caught gazing into green eyes.

"Y-you do?" Nessa finally stammered.

Ailes smiled. "Oh yes, I might even have a secret photo stash of you naked in my room."

Nessa squirmed and tried to lean back, having forgotten she was still standing. *Dammit!*

Ailes laughed and grabbed her by her uninjured arm, pulling her to him and being careful not to brush against her broken arm in its cast. Then he pushed her up against the door and licked her ear while pressing his cock against her softness. She stared at him in shock that he would be so bold.

He kissed her, showing her just how much she affected him, then stepped away, telling her disdainfully, "Don't flatter yourself, Nessa. Now leave before I do something you'll regret." He opened the door then pushed her out and slammed it in her face.

Nessa stared at the door. *What just happened?*

She shook her head then walked back to her car. As she dug her keys from her pocket and got in, she looked up at Ailes' living room window, but the only thing that stared back at her was a lone kitten.

~~*~*

Mike eased forward in the back seat and nudged the woman sitting in the driver's seat in front of him. She sniffed and blubbered incoherent drivel.

"Follow her, or I'll kill her," Mike commanded, putting his knife up against the neck of the little girl sitting next to her.

The woman only cried harder but did as she was told.

They followed Nessa back to her apartment, and Mike watched as she disappeared into the complex.

He caressed his driver's cheek, and she quivered under his touch. "Drive."

"You said you wouldn't hurt us," the woman cried, and in the seat beside her, the little girl began to scream.

"*Drive!*" he yelled.

The woman jumped then put the car into gear, speeding away from the apartment complex.

An hour later, Mike walked out of an alley on the Royal Mile, sucking blood off his fingers as if it were candy. He made the long walk back to Nessa's, the euphoria of the kill making him feel like he was on cloud nine. The thought of the little girl now missing was far from his mind.

It was the perfect feeling for a crisp night like this, and only one thing would make tonight more perfect—the show that awaited him from outside Nessa's window.

~~*~*

Ailes watched as Nessa drove away from the apartment, and then he growled as another car pulled out from the lot and followed. *Damn woman will get herself killed.*

Ailes shook his head. It wasn't his place to worry over her. And yet, before he could stop himself, he had pulled on a shirt, changed out of his sweats, locked the apartment behind him, and had climbed into his car to follow Nessa home.

He easily found the car that had been following Nessa parked just a block away from the woman's apartment complex. He slowly passed it, glancing into the car as he did.

Ailes cursed under his breath then found a place to park a safe distance away.

Mike was in that car, and with him was a woman and child.

Why the hell did you leave the apartment and follow her? he chastised himself.

Ailes looked back at the car and the hostages inside as it pulled away once Nessa was inside her building. He followed, and eventually came to stop outside an alley on the Royal Mile.

Ailes climbed out of the car and ran up the alley. There was Mike, with a gun to the woman's head, pushing her into the wall of a building.

The night gave him cover, and the shadows that Mike had created with his demonic powers shrouded them from view. He could hear the woman's pleas and the girl in the car screaming for her mommy.

Leave them to fate, Ailes.

Ailes turned to walk back to his car.

Shit! Damn conscience.

He turned back around and made his way to the little girl in the car.

Ailes rolled up his sleeves and pressed his fingers to a tattoo on his arm. As it glowed a solid blue, he soon felt a tingling sensation flooding his body. It enabled him, and whomever of his choosing, silence. And boy, did he need it if he was going to get a screaming child out of the car without Mike realizing.

Ailes opened the car door, and the little girl jumped in her car seat and stared at him. She couldn't be no more than four years old. He unbuckled her and quickly pulled her into his arms, putting his finger to his lips to silence her until she was highlighted in blue.

Ailes then ran back toward his car, put her in his back seat, buckled her up, and then climbed into the driver's seat. He looked back toward the alley and weighed his options. He had to save the poor girl's mother.

Before he could react on his decision, though, he heard her scream, and then … silence.

Ailes started the car and quickly put it into gear, driving far away from the Royal Mile.

He looked at the child in the back seat. *Shit! Now I am saddled with a damn kid!*

~~*~*

Nessa clicked between the channels on her television while munching on some crisps. Nearly five hundred channels and nothing was on. What a waste of time.

She turned off the television, stood, and then pulled off her clothes to climb into a hot bath. She sighed as she sunk into the filled tub, making sure her casted, broken arm rested on the edge of the tub. *Maybe it isn't a bad thing that Dad gave me time off.*

Nessa closed her eyes and relaxed further. It had been a long time since she'd had a nice, hot soak.

Her cell phone rang on the sink counter, causing her to jump and slosh water onto the floor. However, she simply shook her head and sank deeper into the tub. Whoever it was, she would call them back later.

Nessa groaned when the phone continued to ring. Finally, having had enough, she climbed out of the tub, dried herself off, and grabbed the damn thing. She looked at the caller I.D. and saw it was from an unknown number, so she put the phone back on the counter and fixed her hair.

The phone rang again. Nessa stared at it. The same unknown number. Whoever it was wanted to get ahold of her badly.

Nessa let it ring a few more times until she got sick of the noise and finally answered with, "What the fuck do you want?"

"First off, foul language isn't a good idea right now, Nessa," Ailes' voice boomed over the phone. "And second, get your ass back to my apartment …"

Nessa heard a child crying in background.

"Shit! Get out of that.

"Nessa get over here now. I need your help." Ailes hung up.

Nessa stared down at her phone. Why in the hell was he calling her? Did he have a child? With whom?

She got dressed and walked out of her apartment toward her car. Before she got to it, though, she stopped and turned to look at the alley beside her building. For a split-second, she had thought she saw a man-sized shadow.

Nessa opened her car door and peered into the back seat, making sure no one had broken in, before quickly climbing in and locking the doors. *I am being too paranoid.*

~~*~*

Ailes picked up the girl and held her away from the nudie magazines that she had found and had started tearing out some of the pages. He hadn't thought the four-year-old would trash his stuff. If anything, he had thought the most she would do was cry for her mother. Nope, she was a wily one and full of energy. It was like she didn't even realize that her mother wasn't there with her.

He put her on the couch when a knock sounded at his door. "You sit there and behave," he told the child as he walked toward the door then opened it.

"Finally," he breathed out in relief.

Nessa looked at him. "What the hell do you want?"

Ailes pulled her inside. "Can we be a little more civil here for a moment, hmm?"

"Civil? You're the one who followed me today, and then you call me?" She shook her head. "I shouldn't have even come. Fuck you, Ailes."

Ailes grabbed Nessa and pulled her toward the living room. "Stop the cursing."

"No. You can't tell me what to do. Now let go of me or, so help me, I will kick your ass!"

Ailes pushed her into the room, and then the two adults stared down at the little girl on the couch who was holding Ailes' kitten.

"Fuck!" the little girl said.

29

Ailes groaned.

Nessa turned to look at him. "Who the heck is that?"

"You need to sit down. I have to tell you something," Ailes said. "But first, can you help me with her?"

"What the fuck do you want me to do?" Nessa whispered, and the little girl repeated after her. Nessa looked at her then back at Ailes. "She has supersonic hearing."

Ailes raised his eyebrows. "Please, just do something. You're a woman … Do womanly stuff."

Nessa blinked a few times. "No, the word you're looking for is *mother*, and I am not hers, nor do I want to be." Nessa frowned. "Where is her mother, anyway?"

"I promise I will tell you. Just please … help me."

The little girl jumped down from the couch and picked up another nudie magazine, beginning to rip the pages from it once more.

Ailes groaned as he walked over and took it from her. When she immediately began to cry, Ailes looked at Nessa.

"Oh, all right, I'll help. But this doesn't change anything between us," Nessa said, picking the girl up and taking her into what could only be Ailes' bedroom.

"What are you doing?"

"Putting her to sleep. Children need to go to bed at this hour. And she's using your bed."

An hour later, Nessa walked out of his bedroom, closing the door softly behind her. She found him in the kitchen, sitting at the table.

Nessa sat down in a chair across from him and stared at him. "Is she yours?"

Ailes looked at her as if she were crazy. "Hell no!"

"Then, whose daughter is she?"

"I don't know," Ailes answered, rubbing his face. "Mike kidnapped them."

Nessa frowned. "Mike? What do you mean?" She wasn't sure she wanted to hear what had happened next. "Ailes, where is her mother?"

"Dead," Ailes replied, and Nessa felt the floor crumble from beneath her. "Mike killed her."

"So, you took her daughter?"

"I had to. She was the only one Mike wasn't paying attention to. You know how it is."

Nessa stood, shaking her head. "No, I don't know how it is. Mike nearly killed me. He is likely stalking me now, and you're saying he kidnapped a little girl and her mother and killed the poor woman? Now you're saying you saved the little girl?"

Ailes looked at her. "I didn't want to save her, but I did. Just like I saved your ass. Everywhere I turn, I am thrown into this shit."

"I didn't ask you to save my ass! And you should have called the police for the girl, not call me over here to put me through this mess you got yourself into."

"Oh, so you're saying you didn't need saving? Not after Mike threw you through your supply cabinet? Or, how about when he broke your arm, hmm?"

Nessa threw her good hand in the air. "I don't need this right now. I'm leaving. Good luck with the kid. And from now on, call the damn police!" Nessa walked toward the door, but before she could open it, Ailes grabbed her good arm and turned her to face him. "Let me go, Ailes."

He stared at her and opened his mouth to say something, but before he could, the little girl began to scream.

Nessa stared at him, wide-eyed, then pulled away as they both ran into the bedroom just as Mike vanished out the window.

"Fucking bastard," Ailes growled, running toward the window and climbing out of it and into his small backyard patio.

Nessa pulled the girl to her and dug out her phone. She started to dial the number to the police, but then hit speed dial for her dad instead. He picked up on the first ring.

"Nessa, what do you need?" Billy asked.

"I had to talk to Ailes at his apartment—"

Her dad swore. "I knew I should have put the files into the computer and locked them with a password," he grumbled.

"Forget about that, Dad. Can you come to Ailes' apartment, please? And quickly. Have Samuel drive you over here. Something's happened." Nessa hung up the phone before he could say anything else then picked up the girl with her good arm, carrying her into the large walk-in closet where she closed the door behind them.

Nessa held her breath as Ailes' front door burst open. The little girl jumped and would have screamed, but Nessa covered her mouth and held her close.

~~*~*

Ailes ran down the block where he thought he had seen Mike run, but the damn bastard was nowhere to be found. He looked around and into the cars parked along the street. *Shit!*

Ailes shook his head then turned to find a cop car parked in front of a diner. He recognized that unmarked car as Brylan's.

He walked into the diner and found Brylan sitting at a table in the corner, drinking a coffee.

Brylan looked up at him as he neared. "What's up?"

"Did you see a man about five four with brown hair, and a blue jumpsuit run near the diner?"

"I haven't seen anyone. Why?"

"Fuck." Ailes brushed his hand through his hair.

His phone buzzed in his pocket, and he dug it out. It was a text from Nessa.

Help! Mike's here. Hiding. Help.

"Fuck!" Ailes yelled then looked at Brylan. "You're coming with me."

~~*~*

Nessa held the little girl close with her good arm and tried to keep from crying out. She could smell an acrid smell, like sulfur, just as she had when Mike had attacked her two days before. That meant he was here. She knew it, just as she knew that he had likely led Ailes away from his apartment to get to her and the girl who she now held in her arms. She would go down fighting.

"Nessa, I know you're hiding. Come out, my love, and bring the little one with you. She can watch our little game," Mike said with a laugh.

Nessa moved the girl farther back into the closet until she was as far as she could get. She felt the coolness of a different doorknob from the one she had used to enter the closet against her back and turned, slowly opening it and peeking out into Ailes' living room. Nessa then put her finger to her lips, and the little girl put her own to hers in understanding.

Nessa bolted from the closet, the little girl clinging to her, and managed to make it out of the apartment just as Mike burst into the closet from the bedroom. She ran as fast as she could, and just as she got out into the street, she saw Ailes and another man she didn't know climbing out of a car.

Nessa ran toward them and managed to get to Ailes as Mike came out of the apartment. He let out a loud roar that sounded like nails scratching a blackboard. Nessa winced, covered the girl's ears, and huddled down as windows from the cars and the buildings around them burst.

Ailes covered Nessa's ears, protecting what was his.

The little girl screamed and cried, jumping as Brylan unloaded his gun.

Nessa watched as the bullets seemed to hurt Mike, but then disappeared into what looked like a cloud of darkness until Mike was no longer there. The roar dissipated with him.

"He's gone," Ailes told them, taking the girl from Nessa before helping her stand.

Nessa nodded at Ailes and looked him over. "What the fuck happened?" she asked, staring at the blood coming out of Ailes' ears.

He also looked pale.

Ailes shook his head. "Not now," he told her as people began to emerge from their homes.

Her dad and Samuel pulled up, parking behind Brylan's car soon after.

Brylan looked at the three of them then just at Ailes. "This is not good," he whispered for only his ears. "The Department of Paranormal Affairs and Investigations will not take this lightly."

Chapter 6

Nessa watched Ailes, who was staring intently at Detective Brylan's car.

Was he thinking about the girl just as much as she was? It seemed so different from the Ailes she knew. Hell, as far as she had always known, he was a whole lot of pissy and self-absorbed. This Ailes, however, was caring and a whole lot of sexy.

Nessa shook her head. *Sexy? Now you're thinking crazy. Since when has Ailes been sexy?*

"The police said they couldn't find Mike at the apartments," her dad told her as he came to stand beside her.

Nessa nodded.

"I think it might be wise if you stay with me or Samuel until this mess blows over."

Nessa looked at her dad. "You think that will stop him from looking for me? Stop him from stalking me?" She nodded toward Ailes' apartment. "He found me there out of all places."

Billy scowled. "I know that, but at least you would have someone to—"

"Don't you dare say *protect you*. I don't need any man to protect me, Dad. And to suggest that I do is downright dirty, not to mention stupid. I can take care of myself. I always have, and I always will." Nessa walked away from her dad and toward the paramedics who were now finished with Ailes and waving her to them.

Billy watched her go then rubbed a hand over his face.

Samuel came to stand beside him. "She always been this stubborn?"

"Aye, ever since she was a wee one." Billy laughed. "Put me through hell, she did, and she has always been so independent and not scared of anything."

Samuel smiled. "Reminds me of my daughter, Meagan. She is stubborn and full of spirit, too. I want to say that she got it from her mother, but that would be a lie. She got hers from her grandfather."

Billy nodded. "I am worried about her, Sam. I don't like her being alone, especially with this mad man out there, stalking her and coming after her. Seems he is stalking Ailes now. Look at the state of his apartment."

"Why stalk her and they not call the cops?" Samuel wondered out loud. He looked at Billy, who nodded as if he wanted to know the same thing. "Who is that little girl to Ailes? Does Ailes have a daughter?"

"No, Ailes doesn't have any children. I don't know who that girl is."

Ailes walked over to them and answered Samuel. "She is my niece," he lied.

Samuel accepted the answer with a nod, but Billy, who knew him well, didn't believe him. It didn't matter. The girl was safe now and would be going to the compound, a place where people who were attacked by the supernatural could be protected. She would be guarded day and night by the Nightingales to keep DPAI off her trail.

The Nightingales were a group of secret officials who protected the paranormal and the non-paranormal world. Most times, they only protected an individual who was connected to the paranormal world, such as being bitten by a vampire or attacked by a being, such as a demon. A fact that Brylan didn't like, because now the Department of Paranormal Affairs and Investigations would be involved.

DPAI worked with the paranormal world, and was a part of the

FBI in America, Scotland Yard, and other law enforcement bureaus around the world. Their motto was, "To protect the affairs and the people of the paranormal world." Not everyone in the paranormal community agreed with their methods or trusted them, though. In fact, it was widely known that there had been corruption within the department since its conception, so it was hard for the paranormal community to accept their help.

"I am sorry about Nessa," Ailes told Billy. "I didn't mean to make it harder for her. I didn't know Mike was stalking her," he continued to lie.

Billy looked at him. "Neither did I. I should have known that he would stalk her. Nessa attacked him, and he didn't press charges."

Ailes nodded and looked at Nessa, who was being treated for the wounds she had received when the glass had shattered around them. If only they knew just what Nessa had gotten into.

He wanted to avoid her like the plague, but just like the little girl who was now on her way to the compound, he found that he couldn't stay away from her, which pissed him off. He was the maker of his own destiny and chose to come and go wherever he pleased. When it came to that woman, though, he couldn't do it. She was a fucking curse. A fucking sexy, beautiful curse.

Mine!

~~*~*

Later that night, Nessa sat in front of her computer. The search that she had been conducting for the last hour on Mike hadn't yielded any results. It was like the man didn't exist.

She rubbed her hands over her face and thought back to the night she had first met him. What about him had stood out to her? What about him had been different? Her memories were fuzzy at best, and most of them were about the violence that she had received from him.

Nessa closed her eyes and thought back to the restaurant that she had met him at. She had smiled at the regulars, and then Mike had come in.

She remembered thinking lewd comments when she had seen him and thinking about what had been under that mechanic's coveralls that he had been wearing.

Nessa's eyes snapped open, and she brought up a new search. The coveralls had had his name on it, and the name of the place he had said he worked at—Stu's Garage and Tire.

Nessa typed in the name and found the garage's website. There was a picture of the founders, and in it stood Mike. But he didn't look like the Mike who had attacked her. This Mike had darker hair, and his complexion seemed bright and full of life. The Mike she knew was pale, like the life had been sucked out of him.

Nessa wrote down the name and address of the garage into her phone then shut down the computer. She would go there tomorrow and ask about him. Maybe she could get his address and give it to Detective Brylan. Surely Brylan had enough for a search warrant. After all, Mike had stalked her, attacked and killed a woman, and broke into Ailes' apartment.

Nessa walked into her room and to the window, closing the blinds. At least, to herself, she could admit that she was scared shitless.

She climbed into bed and stared at the ceiling, trying to force herself to relax enough to go to sleep.

~~*~*

Nessa bolted up from her bed a couple of hours later, the sounds of movement outside her window having woken her up.

She swallowed as a shadow passed her window, and then she grabbed the gun that she kept in her nightstand drawer. If Mike had come to take her, she would shoot his ass first.

Nessa climbed out of bed then walked slowly to the window, jumping when the figure knocked on the glass. Why would Mike take the time to knock on the damn window?

Nessa pulled back the drapes and pointed the gun at the man standing before her.

"Fucking hell, Nessa. Where the hell did you get a gun?" Ailes roared at her.

Nessa lowered the weapon. "Why the hell are you outside my fucking window?"

Ailes shrugged. "I guess I wanted to make sure Mike wasn't hiding around here. Can you please let me in? It's cold out here."

Nessa put the gun back in the nightstand drawer then opened the window to allow Ailes to climb into her bedroom. "Ever hear of knocking on the damn door?"

"I did, but you were asleep," Ailes said, closing the window then locking it. "You need to keep this locked at all times."

"It doesn't lock. It's broken," Nessa informed him, looking at the clock. "Six in the morning and already I'm dealing with overprotective assholes."

Ailes growled, "Don't think for a minute that I came to protect your ass. I was just doing a favor for Billy."

Nessa looked at him. "Yeah, he's the overprotected ass, and you are his asshat minion. Why would you care what happens to me, anyway?"

"I don't care, but Billy is my friend, and I help my friends when they ask."

Nessa walked out of the bedroom and into the kitchen, Ailes following her. She grabbed the coffee pot and put a few scoops of coffee grounds into the machine.

"He paid you to come here, didn't he?"

Ailes' silence was enough of an answer for her.

She turned to look at him and to tell him to get out of her apartment, but she found him staring at her computer. Had she left it on? She could have sworn she had shut it down before bed.

Nessa walked over to see what Ailes was looking at and froze.

She was on the screen, asleep. It was a video of her in bed, naked. And on another window screen, there were photos of her naked in the shower and walking around her apartment, all flicking, one by one, in a slide show.

Nessa moved to delete them from the computer, but Ailes stopped her.

"It's evidence. You can't delete them."

"The hell I can't!" Nessa tried to move him away from the computer.

"No, Nessa, you can't. If Mike put them on the computer, he might have put them there with a virus. It would be foolish to try to delete them."

Nessa finally got him to move and began deleting the pictures from her hard drive. But, just as Ailes had said, more began to show up until her computer was covered in photos of her naked, of her sleeping, bathing, eating. A video popped up next, and she watched in horror as Mike lay down in the bed next to her as she slept. He played with her hair and smelled it then laughed as he touched her face. The time stamp read it was from just last night.

"Fuck you!" Nessa screamed, pushing the computer off her desk. It fell and the screen broke, but the video kept playing.

Ailes grabbed Nessa and pulled her into the living room, holding her tightly as he called Brylan.

~~*~*

Brylan walked back into the apartment after he had put the computer, its tower, and the evidence his team had found in his car. He crouched down in front of Nessa, who sat on the couch, staring into space. "Do you think he did anything to you last night?" Brylan asked.

"No, I am okay. I mean, I don't think he did anything," Nessa said, putting her head into her hands. "Oh God."

Brylan nodded then stood and left her in the living room to find Ailes, who was in the bedroom, staring down at the bed then looking at the window then back at the bed.

"Do you know how Mike could have gotten into the room?"

Brylan asked.

Ailes nodded and walked to the window. "Nessa said the lock on this is broken. She's right; it doesn't lock." He slid the lock shut then showed that he could still open the window.

"He waited and timed it perfectly, Ailes. He knew you would be here this morning," Brylan said.

"He was watching."

Brylan nodded. "She isn't safe here. It would be wise to move her to the compound. The Nightingales can protect her more than you can."

Ailes looked at him. His woman was not going to the compound. He would protect her as much as he could. She was his, whether he wanted to admit or not.

Mine!

Chapter 7

Nessa walked to Hellish after Ailes and Detective Brylan had left her apartment. She had packed a few things and left them with Brylan, who had told her that he would drop them off at her dad's apartment down the hall from hers so she could go to work. She didn't want to admit that she was scared. She didn't want to move in with her dad, either. She hadn't lived with the old man since she had been sixteen. She loved her dad, but sometimes they didn't get along.

Nessa passed the bus stop and came to a stop. Something in her gut told her not to look up, but she found herself doing so, anyway.

Across the street, stood Mike, who smiled at her and waved.

Nessa shook her head and bolted. She ran as fast as she could until the gates of Hellish came into view. She turned to look behind her but didn't see Mike. Where was he?

She turned back around and ran face-first into someone's chest. Nessa screamed and began to fight the hands that grabbed her.

"Nessa, will you shut the hell up?" she heard Ailes say in his deep voice.

Nessa stopped fighting and stared into Ailes' handsome face. Boy, was she relieved or what? She took in a gulp of air and tried to calm down.

"I'm sorry. I didn't mean to," Nessa said as she looked around.

Ailes followed her gaze but saw no one besides the tourists who were always walking around the Royal Mile.

"Mike was following me. I saw him at the bus stop, and I could have sworn he was chasing me," she explained.

Ailes didn't say anything, just stared at her.

"I'm not crazy. He was right behind me."

"I believe you, Nessa." How could he not? Mike had broken into her apartment and had had the audacity to lay next to her in her own bed.

He would kill the demon for touching his woman.

Nessa nodded. Not that she cared that he believed her.

She closed her eyes in embarrassment at the thought that he had seen the damn video and photos of her. God, the photos … Ailes had seen her naked.

Pulling away from him, she walked into Hellish, and Ailes followed her.

Nessa unlocked her workroom and turned on the lights. She looked around the room, in the cupboards, and then in the room that Samuel was using for his workspace. She then walked around the whole parlor, checking her dad's space, the supply closet, the stairs that led up to the apartment above, the office, and the bathrooms. She let out a relieved sigh when she found no one there but her and Ailes. Then she looked at him.

"What do you want, Ailes?"

"To tell you that you might want to think about going into witness protection," he told her.

"Oh, so you came here to tell me that?" Nessa walked back to the front of the parlor and began to work on reorganizing her workroom, which was going to take forever one-handed. There was too much work to be done if she was going to come back to work. Her cupboard was still broken in spots, her ink was everywhere, and she would need to use the parlor's computer to order herself a new tattoo gun since she couldn't use the one that she had attacked Mike with.

"Nessa, you are in danger. And I didn't come here just to say that. I came here hoping you would listen to reason."

"No, you came here to tell me to listen to your detective friend, because you want me to run."

"No, I don't want you to run," Ailes growled. Gods, his woman was infuriating, and that attracted him to her. Why couldn't he just leave her alone?

"Well, then you don't mind if I tell you to get the hell out of my parlor, and then tell you again that I don't need your help," Nessa said. "I can take care of myself."

Ailes shook his head, walking out of the parlor and from Nessa. He didn't need this shit. She was a grown woman, and if she was going to be stubborn about this, then he was going to just leave her to her own. She didn't even want his help. Then again, he could tell just how afraid she truly was. She would never admit it, though. No, Nessa would have to be kidnapped just so she could see the seriousness of the danger that she was now in. Damn, he wasn't liking where this was heading.

~~*~*

A few hours later, Nessa finished up in her workroom then locked it up. She had ordered her new tattoo gun from her phone. It would arrive Thursday at the parlor. She even ordered herself a new, spiffy chair and cupboard for her new inks. All in all, despite the stalker, the day was going great.

She locked up Hellish for the day and decided it was time to take a drive to the car garage that Mike worked at. She needed to know if he was there and maybe call Brylan so Mike could be arrested and taken off the streets.

Nessa walked to the parking lot where her car was parked and found Ailes standing beside the vehicle. She groaned. What the hell did he want now?

"I don't have time for you, Ailes. I have an appointment at the mechanics," she told him as she unlocked the car.

Ailes looked at the vehicle. "Funny, I don't see anything wrong with it." He walked over to the passenger side and climbed in. "I

44

guess I could go with you to make sure you don't get swindled or something."

Nessa scowled. "You're not going anywhere with me."

"No? Well, I guess you're not leaving either."

Nessa shook her head and climbed into the driver's seat. She tried to start the car, but it didn't make a sound. It didn't even turn over.

"Unbelievable. What the hell did you do to my car?" she yelled.

Ailes shook his head as he climbed out then walked to the front of it. "I didn't do a damn thing to it. Pop the hood."

Nessa did as she was told, and he looked under it and chuckled. The battery was gone. Billy must have taken it out last night. "No battery, Nessa."

"What do you mean *no battery*?" Nessa climbed out of the car and looked under the hood. "What the hell!" She was so pissed. "Dad, you motherfuckin' arsehole!"

Ailes tried not to laugh when her Scottish accent seeped into her normally cool English one. It was sexy as hell, just like the woman herself.

Ailes shook his head. *Shut the hell up!* He needed to think with his brain, not his dick.

"Where were you going?" Ailes asked, trying to push his lewd thoughts away.

Nessa looked at him, weighing her options. now she didn't have a car to get to Stu's, yet here stood a man who frankly infuriated her and seemed to follow her just as much as Mike did. He had a car, though, so he could take her. But, then she would have to tell him everything she had found when she had searched for information about Mike last night. He would be the first to likely tell her to give the information to Brylan and go into witness protection, where he wanted her. Then again, Ailes might help her. Either way, she didn't see any other way out of it. Ailes would follow her, anyway, and then her dad would likely find out. The old man already didn't think she could take care of herself.

Nessa looked at Ailes, her mind made up. "Stu's Garage. It's eleven blocks from Hellish," Nessa told him. "Mike works there."

"All right, let's go," Ailes said.

"Really?"

"Yeah."

Nessa was shocked that Ailes agreed to drive her. Hell, he didn't even tell her that she was crazy. No, Ailes just told her to climb into his car and that he would take her. No muss, no fuss.

He wasn't worried about her? Even a little bit?

For some reason, that thought made her heart tighten, but she didn't know why.

~~*~*

They pulled into Stu's parking lot then climbed out of the car and walked into the small garage. The smell of oil, and the sound of power tools filled the air around them.

Nessa found the manager sitting at a desk. He was fat, his face and hair covered in car oil, and his coveralls were dirty from working on cars. He looked at her, his eyes dark pools of coal, and she shivered. Something about the man was off.

Ailes stared intently at him and shook his head. The man shrank back a little.

Nessa looked at the two men. Did they know each other?

"What can I do for you?" the man asked.

Nessa rested her casted arm on the counter and said, "I am looking for Mike. I was told he works here. He fixed my car, and now it's broken again. I need to know if he can come to my house and fix it."

"No house visits allowed, miss. And if you want to talk to Mike, I can get him for you." The man grunted as he stood then walked out from behind the desk and past them.

Nessa quickly covered her mouth and nose as the pungent smell of decaying flesh hit her. Damn, when was the last time the manager had bathed?

46

Ailes seemed unfazed, simply staring after the man. However, as the manager disappeared into the back, Ailes turned toward her and said, "We need to leave, Nessa. Now."

"Hell no! I am not leaving until I know for sure that Mike indeed works here," Nessa told him.

"Nessa, this isn't a good idea. We need to leave. Don't make me carry you out."

"What are you talking about? You drove me here, and you didn't seem to care when we parked and came in to talk to him."

"That was before I saw him. Before …" Ailes shut his mouth as the man came back with another man in tow.

"Before what?" Nessa whispered then followed Ailes' gaze to the two men.

Nessa frowned. He looked like Mike, but he wasn't Mike. How could that be?

"Hello. My uncle tells me that you're looking for me?" He smiled at Nessa. "I don't believe I have met you before, young lady. If I had, I would certainly have remembered a fine-ass woman like you."

Ailes swallowed and stared at the two men. The younger one smiled back, his eyes turning from bright blue to deep black.

"She made a mistake. She thought this was where she got her car fixed," Ailes told them then turned to Nessa and took her by the arm.

"Come on, honey; we need to get to our date. Let's leave the nice men to their business." He pulled her out of the garage, keeping her close to his side. "Don't look back and keep walking. Once we are in the car, I want you to buckle up and not argue with me."

Nessa opened her mouth then shut it when a loud screech came from the garage.

"Shit! Run!" Ailes hissed, pulling her into a mad dash toward his car.

They got in just as a man from the shop crawled onto the hood of Ailes' car.

"What the hell is that?" Nessa screamed.

Ailes threw the car in reverse and ran into the man from the front desk. He winced when he felt the sickening thud under his car.

"Oh my God!"

Ailes looked at Nessa, who was pointing at the man in front of them. His head was nearly off his shoulders.

Ailes put the car into drive and pressed his foot on the gas, speeding away. The men ran after them.

"Shit!" Ailes said as one caught up to them.

Nessa screamed as the man smiled at her as he ran beside the car, his mouth wide open, revealing sharp teeth.

Ailes growled then pulled up the sleeve of his right arm. He brought his knees up to the steering wheel to steady the vehicle as he touched the tattoo nestled in the crook of his arm. It glowed green, illuminating the car and the light outside.

The man screamed and fell back. Ailes watched from the rearview mirror as the man rolled on the ground, enveloped in green, purifying light and became a dot in the horizon as he sped away.

"What the fuck was that?" Nessa asked when they were a safe distance away from the garage. "Ailes, what the fuck is going on?"

"You should have listened to me when I told you that we had to leave. Why don't you ever fucking listen to a damn thing anyone tells you?" Ailes yelled.

"Stop the car."

"No."

"Dammit, Ailes, stop the car!"

Ailes slammed on the brakes and unlocked the doors. "There, you happy? Leave. I don't care. Get yourself killed."

Nessa opened the door and climbed out of the car. She turned to give Ailes a piece of her mind, but before she could open her mouth, he closed the door and sped off, surprisingly leaving her in front of her apartment building, alone.

What the hell had just happened? Who were those people? *What* were they? Had he just pulled a tattoo from his arm?

Chapter 8

Ailes burst into Brylan's office just as the detective sat down. "Very nice of you to come by, Ailes." He looked at the door that now stood on its side. "You'll be paying for that."

"Stupid fucking woman," Ailes growled. "I should have never listened to her. All she does is get me deeper into this fucking mess!"

Brylan cleared his throat and pointed to a closed door beside the room.

Ailes stared at him.

"There is a child present."

"You have got to be kidding me?" Ailes growled. "She's in the room right now?"

Ignoring him, Brylan said, "Nessa called me and told me quite the story about a few mechanics climbing walls and being covered in green lights. Oh, and that you ran over a man with your car."

Ailes narrowed his eyes. "You didn't say anything, did you?"

Brylan shook his head. Then he stood and went to the door, opening it. The little girl came walking out, rubbing the tiredness from her face. Brylan picked her up and smiled at the child he held.

"I have to get her to Ellas. She has agreed to take her in with the other children. Your sister has quite the heart to take in so many children."

Ailes growled, following him out of the building and to his vehicle. "What do I do about Nessa? Mike's family clearly knows about her by now, and you know that they will be claiming she killed one of their own yesterday."

Brylan shut the door to the back seat. "Why her? Didn't you have something to do with what happened yesterday, as well?" Brylan climbed into the driver's side, started the car, and then rolled down the window. "I told you to either take her to the compound to Mikalio or to Isla's house. Either way, this is a job for a Nightingale. And last time I checked, you are one." With that parting shot, Brylan raised his window and pulled out of the parking lot.

The little girl in the back seat waved at Ailes as they disappeared.

~~*~*

Mike looked around the garage parking lot where the body had been moments before.

"We tried to get her, Lenarska. The half-blood was protecting her."

Mike looked at him and smiled. "Don't worry, Ariskar; you did well." He patted the other man on the shoulder then grabbed him by the neck, squeezing it as he lifted him in the air. "Say hello to the others for me."

Ariskar screamed as a black shadow seeped out of his body and blew apart.

Mike threw the empty husk down at the feet of the other men standing before him. "Anyone else want to follow Ariskar?"

The men shook their heads.

"Good. Now get back to work. I want her, and I expect you will do a better job this time. Kill the half-blood and bring Nessa to me."

"What about Elder Kainez?" one of them dared to ask.

Mike looked at him. "What about him?" he hissed.

"We were told not to follow your orders. We are to report to him straight away … and to Lariska."

Mike grabbed him by the neck and squeezed. "Elder Kainez will never know. You report to me from now on."

"Lenarska, you will unhand him this instant," a female voice boomed throughout the room.

The men huddled into the shadows, and the man whom Mike now held whimpered.

Mike laughed, dropping the man onto his butt. The man scuttled into a dark corner along with the others.

"Lariska, so happy to see you," Mike said to the beautiful woman with long black hair walking in from the back of the garage.

"Elder Kainez is not pleased with you, brother," Lariska told him. "In fact, he has requested that you come to him."

"And come to him, I shall."

"Now." Lariska grabbed him around his neck, and Mike screamed as they were engulfed in hot flames.

Lariska threw Mike down onto the ground at the feet of Elder Kainez.

Kainez chuckled. "Quite the entrance, Black Death."

Lariska smiled and bowed.

Mike tried to catch his breath as he pulled himself to his feet, but then Elder Kainez knocked him back down with a kick of his boot.

Kainez stepped on Mike's head, pressing the demon's face against the glass floor where he could see his kin being murdered over and over again in the room below. That was the fate that awaited a demon if they didn't follow Elder Kainez's orders. It didn't matter if they were part of the royal family or not.

"Do you feel the pain, Lenarska?" Kainez asked. "Hear the screams of your brothers?"

Mike growled and dared not move. Kainez was stronger than him. Hell, he was stronger than his own father.

"That is what awaits you for opening up our world to a human," Kainez told him. "Now, because of your mess and idiocy, we have to rectify it and send out the cleaning crew. The Nightingales are likely on our scent, and all because of your obsession with that human girl." Kainez pressed Mike's face and body further into the floor until Mike's fragile human body began to struggle for air and bones began to break.

He wouldn't dare leave the body. If he did and went back to his demon form, Kainez would trap him in whatever vessel he had at his disposal. He would be doomed.

"Lariska will assist you in cleaning this little mishap of yours up. You will leave the human woman alone and do as you are told. Do I make myself clear?"

"Yes, master," Mike wheezed.

Elder Kainez lifted his foot off Mike, and Mike took in a great gulp of air.

Kainez laughed. "He is all yours, Black Death, my beauty. Take him from my sight."

Lariska bowed then picked up her brother from off the ground, dragging him from the elder demon's room.

Once out of the building and away from the elder did Mike dare to attack his sister.

"I will kill you," he hissed, but Lariska only laughed.

"You can try."

Mike punched her, but his fist only hit air. "Fuck you, bitch!"

Lariska shook her head. "Too bad that famous anger of yours didn't come in handy. We could have used it back home."

"That place will never be my home. You can rot there for all I care."

"If your body weren't filled with magic, I would say that you could rot as well, but surprisingly, that body of yours is perfect. How do you do it?" Lariska grabbed Mike by the neck and pulled him to her. "Don't fool me, brother. I know what you are doing, and I know all your plans. You will do as Elder Kainez says. I can easily end your pitiful existence. Leave the girl and do as you're told." She threw him to the ground at her feet.

Done with the message, Lariska's form dissipated, and Mike was left sitting there, beginning to smell like death. He screamed and blew a tree closest to him from its roots and to the ground. Then he stood and walked down the street.

He would have her. Elder Kainez couldn't keep him from Nessa.

"Would you like a fun time, sweetheart? I can take that anger from you," a woman's voice crooned from an alleyway.

Mike turned and looked at the human woman who stood there with her shirt lifted, her bare breasts showing in the rays of the moonlight above.

Mike growled. If he couldn't have Nessa, he could have this one.

He walked toward her and, as he got closer, the woman screamed.

~~*~*

Lariska watched as her brother took the unconscious human and carried her into a warehouse, disappearing inside. Then she pulled out the tablet that she always carried, and Elder Kainez's face appeared.

"I have found where he has his human concubines. Should I send in the team?"

"No, Black Death, let him have his fun. They will be dead soon enough. Come back to the house, my beloved."

Lariska hung up. "Soon, brother, you, too, will feel the black death."

Chapter 9

One month later, Nessa stared at an invitation that Samuel had just handed her. "A Halloween party?"

"Yes, it's for my daughter's birthday. She flies in tomorrow morning. I want her to be surprised," Samuel told her. "Please come."

Nessa sighed. "Fine, I will go. But I won't be happy about it."

The doorbell jingled, and they both looked toward the front door to find Ailes walking into Hellish.

Nessa groaned. Mr. Grumpy, Sexy Pants was back.

Samuel pulled out another invitation and handed it to Ailes.

Oh God. Why him?

Nessa tried not to say anything. It was Samuel's party after all.

"I'm sorry. I don't go to parties," Ailes said, staring at Nessa.

"Nonsense. This is a birthday slash Halloween party. Nessa is going," Samuel tacked that last line on, knowing the man would change his mind.

"Is she?" Ailes asked.

Samuel nodded. "If anything, there will be other girls at the party. Maybe you will find one you like and take her home with you." Samuel winked.

"Strippers?"

"Male and female," Samuel said with a chuckle and another wink.

Nessa's eyes widened. "I thought you said this was a party for your daughter?"

"It is, but Meagan is twenty-eight. Besides, she likes that stuff. You know—strippers, costumes, alcohol. She is a party girl. She won't mind." Samuel patted them both on the shoulders. "Now, don't forget to wear a costume. This year's theme is sexy, so you must find the skimpiest, sexiest costume you can." He smiled at them then disappeared into the back of the parlor.

"Well, I guess I better get on a banana hammock then," Ailes commented.

Nessa stared at him. "A what?"

"You know, the underwear that …"

Nessa shook her head and walked away, leaving Ailes chuckling. Seeing her frazzled and shocked made him hard.

He would go to the party, but only because she would be there in her skimpiest outfit.

~~*~*

Nessa turned around and around, looking at the sexy kitty costume she had chosen for the Halloween party. She had used some dye to make her red highlights more pronounced and deemed herself ready. Good thing she no longer had that damn cast on her arm.

Leaving her apartment, Nessa stared at her dad's apartment door and considered asking him again if he wanted to go to the party with her. Then she decided against it. Her dad didn't like parties as much as he preferred to keep away so he stayed sober.

Nessa left the building and drove to the parking lot behind Hellish. She went in through the back door and up the stairs where she knocked on the door.

Samuel greeted her with a smile and a warm hug. "Happy Halloween, Nessa!" Samuel said. "Come in."

"Happy Halloween, Samuel," Nessa returned as she made her way to the small breakfast bar that Samuel had set up with cups, alcohol, and Jell-O shots.

"Do you want a drink?"

"A beer if you have one," Nessa answered.

Samuel went into the kitchen then came back with two cold beers. He handed one to her and invited her to sit down.

"The apartment looks great," she said, looking around. "Better than when Jimbo was in it."

Samuel nodded and took a drink of his beer. "It was filthy in here, but with Marlow's help, I got it cleaned."

Nessa looked at him. "Who is Marlow?"

Samuel smiled and blushed. "Well, he … he and I are …"

Nessa blinked and put her beer down on the table. "Samuel, are you gay?"

"Yes," Samuel replied. "Marlow is my boyfriend. Meagan just adores him."

"Wow. How long have you been seeing him?" Nessa asked.

"Only a week. And you're taking this surprisingly well. The last parlor I worked for had a problem with me."

Nessa shrugged. "It doesn't matter to me if you're gay. Does Dad know?"

Samuel shook his head. "Didn't tell him, but I suspect he already knows. Hard to pull the wool over your old man's eyes."

Nessa laughed. "Dad used to say he had eyes in the back of his head."

"So, how did you come by having a daughter? Did you adopt Meagan?"

Samuel smiled. "No, she is my daughter from my previous marriage. I wasn't always gay, but I kind of knew deep down I was. Meagan was fifteen when we divorced. That's when I found out I was gay. She will be staying with me while she is back in college." Samuel looked down at his watch. "Look at the time, I have to go make sure everyone is comfortable." Samuel stood. "Meagan is in her room. Can you tell her that the guests are here?" He excused himself to let in the guests that began to arrive.

"Sure." Nessa got up and walked to the spare bedroom, knocking on the door. When no one answered, she opened it, causing Meagan to nearly jump out of her boots.

"I am so sorry. Your dad told me to come get you."

"Sorry. Didn't hear you knock. Can you zip me up?" Meagan pointed at the zipper to her short burlesque costume.

Nessa closed the door behind her and walked over to her, helping her zip it up. That was when she noticed the hearing aids.

"You're deaf?" Nessa blurted.

Meagan looked at her. "Yes, it's no big deal."

"I am sorry. I am an ass. What I meant to say was that you're deaf and I am the idiot who knocked on the door," Nessa explained.

"It's really no big deal, and I would appreciate it if you didn't tell anyone that I'm deaf." Meagan let her hair down from the towel she wore on her head. Her hair was a bright red and really curly. It clashed with her pale, freckled skin and green eyes. She was beautiful, but no one would know she was Samuel's daughter because she didn't have not one of his features.

Nessa pretended to lock her mouth and throw away the key. "No one will know."

Meagan laughed. "Listen, I am not ashamed of being deaf. I just don't want people to look at me and do the *oh, poor thing* look," she explained. "I got that enough back in Texas with my mom and her friends."

~~*~*

Ailes walked into the apartment and was greeted by a smiling Samuel.

"Happy Halloween, Ailes! Glad you could make it!"

Ailes nodded and handed him a case of beer. "I figured you had enough, but I wanted the harder stuff."

"I ran out of the harder stuff a while ago, so this is great," Samuel said then looked him over. "I like your costume. Sexy and dapper."

Ailes looked down at his suit. It wasn't too sexy. He didn't find it too revealing either, not like the other people at the party. But it suited him better than showing skin ever would. Besides, he would probably have to explain why his tattoos glowed.

"Nessa is with my daughter in her room. You can sit wherever you like."

Ailes nodded then walked into the living room and found a wall as far from people as he could get. He perked up when Nessa walked out of the spare bedroom with a red, curly-haired beauty.

Nessa was dressed up like a cat. Her fishnet stockings disappeared under a short skirt, and her breasts were pushed up by a corset. He readjusted himself and tried to push away the naked images he had of her.

He took a draw off his beer and walked out onto the patio to the cold air of Scotland. Maybe this had been a bad idea.

~~*~*

An hour later, the party was in full swing, and the guests were drunk, rowdy, and having fun.

The noise from the music and laughter circled Nessa as she made her way from Meagan to the patio to get some fresh air. She wobbled on drunken legs as she fumbled for the sliding door and finally managed to walk out onto the patio. She wasn't alone.

Ailes sat on one of the chairs, his arms behind his head as he stared at the night sky above.

Nessa smiled. "Hey sexy, broody butt," she slurred, walking over to him and plopping down onto his lap.

Ailes stared at her. The smell of alcohol was evident on her breath. "Excuse me?"

"You heard what I said." Nessa laughed and grabbed the lapels of his suit. "This is supposed to be sexy? Where is the skin?" She lifted one of her legs. "I'm sexy, and I'm showing skin. You should, too. Here, I will help you." Nessa unbuttoned his shirt until the top of his chest lay bare. She sighed as she rubbed it with her hand.

Ailes groaned. It took all of his willpower not to lift her skirt, rip off those fish nets, and take her right there on the patio. Instead, he took her hands in his and gently put them on her lap. "I think you may have had too much to drink, Nessa. Let me help you to your apartment."

Nessa laughed. "You didn't drink enough." She giggled again. "But I will let you take me to my apartment." She stood, and Ailes had to grab her before she fell into the railing and right off the patio.

"Come on, Nessa; let's get you somewhere safe." He walked her into the apartment, past Samuel who looked concerned, and outside to his car. He deposited her in the passenger seat and shut the door.

"Is she all right?" Samuel asked, walking over to him, hand in hand with a handsome, brown-haired man.

"Just had too much to drink. I'm taking her someplace where she can sober up and be safe," Ailes explained then nodded at the man beside Samuel.

"This is Marlow," Samuel said, and Marlow smiled. "Let me know if you need me, and we can come get Nessa."

"She will be in good hands." That said, Ailes climbed into his car and sped away.

He pulled into the driveway of Brylan's house thirty minutes later and helped Nessa out of the car. Then Ailes helped her into the house and upstairs to one of the spare bedrooms. He hadn't meant to take her here but going back to her apartment and leaving her alone was a bad idea, and his apartment was still trashed. His kitten, Thor, mewled at his ankles for food. *So not the time right now, Thor.*

Ailes helped Nessa out of her costume while she kept trying to dance with him and instantly regretted it. She was naked underneath. He groaned and tried to keep his hands to himself as he led her to the bed.

Nessa giggled as she fell onto the bed and grabbed him around the neck, pulling him on top of her and bringing his lips to hers. The kiss lasted for a while until Ailes broke away and looked at Nessa.

"I want you, Ailes," she whimpered as she wrapped her legs around his waist.

Ailes shook his head. He wanted her, too, but not like this.

He unwrapped her legs from around his waist then covered her up. "Go to sleep, Nessa."

"Okay," she said and promptly fell asleep.

What the hell had he been thinking?

Chapter 10

He could have watched her all day as she slept, but right now, he needed to think with his brain and not another part of his body. Ailes hadn't left her for fear that she would need help.

Nessa moaned and turned over in her sleep. The covers slid down to reveal a beautiful breast and a rosy nipple. Ailes closed his eyes and tried not to groan.

It was time to go. He had stayed as long as he could. But before he departed, he left a note, a hair of the dog, pain pills, and a tray of breakfast on the nightstand beside the bed.

Nessa woke an hour later, finding the drink and pills. She took them, relieved that her pounding head would soon stop.

She looked around. Hadn't Ailes been with her? She looked underneath the blanket and tried not to panic. Had they done anything while they were drunk? Oh God, she hoped not.

Wait. This wasn't her home. Where was she?

Nessa climbed out of bed and found a pair of jeans and a T-shirt. Then she opened the bedroom door, and Ailes fell into the room, having fallen asleep in the hallway.

"What the hell? Warn a man before you open a door on him," Ailes said, pissed at himself for not being more careful.

"I wouldn't need to if you weren't asleep outside a woman's door." Nessa looked up and down the hallway. "Where are we?"

Ailes stood, running his hand through his long, black hair. "Brylan's home."

"Why are we here? Why didn't you take me home?"

"I didn't want you to be alone. You were drunk," Ailes explained.

Aww, so sweet, a thought said, and she promptly told it to shut up.

"I don't care what you wanted. You should have taken me home. My dad would have helped me."

"While you were naked? Don't you think he would have wondered why his daughter was naked and dancing with me?"

Nessa's face went red. "W-well, that could have been fixed. I would have told him that I was preparing for a bath."

Ailes laughed. "A bath? I don't think you could convince Billy that you were going to bathe."

"Shut up and take me home."

"Fine, but eat first," Ailes told her.

Nessa sat down on the bed and ate as quickly as she could.

Ailes laughed then motioned for her to follow him downstairs when she was done.

As he drove, Ailes looked over at Nessa. "Do you want to go to a concert tonight?"

"With you?" Was he asking her on a date?

"Yes, with me. Who else would ask you to a concert?"

Nessa rolled her eyes. "You never know. I could have gone with Samuel."

Ailes laughed. "Are you going with me or not?"

Nessa looked at him and finally sighed. Those handsome green and yellow eyes got to her. *Oh God.* "I would be happy to go with you. But this isn't a date, you got that?"

Ailes chuckled as he pulled into her parking lot and let her out.

He smiled and called out to her, "By the way, wear something rock and goth if you can."

~~*~*

Four hours later, Nessa found herself walking into the Dark Angel Chapel. It wasn't a church, just called that by the goth who danced in front of her. It was a bar, which held a dance floor and rooms for people to socialize and drink. It was dark and had many lights flashing as people danced on the dance floor.

Nessa spotted Ailes moving through the crowd toward her.

"Like it?" he asked when he finally stood before her.

Nessa looked him up and down. He wore leather pants and a vest that showed a muscled chest and belly. His chest was covered in rune-like tattoos. God, he looked yummy.

Shut up, shut up. Think of an old lady if you have to. This isn't a freaking date, and you are definitely not going home with him.

When Ailes was called to the stage over the speakers, he smiled and told her, "Gotta go. The booth is right next to the stage. It's reserved for us." Ailes then turned on his heels and pushed through the crowd toward the stage.

What the hell was he doing? And what did he mean by *us*?

Nessa decided to do as she was told and found the booth relatively easy because, to her surprise, Samuel and another man—she didn't recall his name—sat there as well.

"Nessa, glad you made it," Samuel said, pulling her in for a hug. "How are you? When Ailes took you from the party, we were so worried."

"I'm all right. He didn't hurt me. He let me sleep it off at Detective Brylan's home, which I think Ailes might be living at since his apartment is kind of trashed. What are you doing here?"

"Ailes invited Marlow and me to his concert."

"*His* concert?" Nessa snorted. "I doubt it."

"He is a famous rock star, known throughout Europe. You didn't know?" Marlow asked.

When Nessa shook her head, Samuel and Marlow both said, "Gasp," at the same time.

How the hell hadn't she known that? Wouldn't his picture have been plastered all over the place?

"Oh, girl, you need to watch Ailes. You won't be disappointed," Marlow said.

"Sorry for being so rude. I'm Marlow." He pulled her in for a hug.

"Ailes is very handsome," Marlow said. "You should sleep with him."

Samuel looked at Marlow. "Remember what we talked about last night?"

"Pft, as if I could forget," Marlow said. "No more matchmaking."

"I like you, Marlow, and I would prefer not to have to kick your ass," Nessa warned.

"Fine, but the least you could do is dance with him after the concert," Marlow said. "Until then"—he grabbed her hand and pulled her out onto the dance floor—"dance with me."

Marlow and Nessa danced until the song ended, and then they took their seats at the booth just as Ailes came on the stage. He winked at Nessa then began to sing.

Nessa was floored by his voice and the song that told the story of a lass who had come upon a man, and the man fell in love with her and was rejected. It was a sad song and tugged at her heart.

He looked sexy and handsome up there, his tattoos glowing brightly in the darkness, just as they had that day at the car garage. They had to be glow in the dark ink. She would ask her dad.

The concert dragged on until late that night as he sang some songs that she actually knew, requested from the large audience that had formed around the stage.

When Ailes finished, he walked through the crowd and finally joined them at the booth. He sat next to Nessa, who squirmed at the smell of his cologne and vanilla shampoo that made her wish she could bathe in him.

"Did you enjoy yourselves?" he asked Samuel and Marlow.

"Oh yes," Marlow said, biting his straw.

"A stunning performance," Samuel said, swatting Marlow on the shoulder, which made Marlow laugh.

Ailes turned to Nessa. "What about you?"

"It was fine, I guess," Nessa said, taking a sip of her rum and Coke that Samuel had gotten her.

"You didn't like it?"

"I liked it," Nessa said.

Marlow winked at her cheekily. It was as if he could read her mind and was taunting her to do something about it.

I am not sleeping with him, her eyes said.

Marlow frowned, his eyes asking, *Why not?*

Because he is not my type.

Liar! Marlow coughed and turned his attention to Samuel. "I think it's time we leave. It was nice seeing you, Nessa." He stood and gave her a hug, whispering, "Just do it, chicken."

Samuel hugged her and looked at Ailes. "Are you going to be okay with him? We can give you a ride."

Marlow snorted. "She is a gown woman, my dear. She will be fine with Ailes. You have nothing to worry about."

"He's right; go home. I will be all right," she told Samuel, but the worried look in his eyes did not dissipate.

Samuel nodded at Ailes then walked out of the bar, hand in hand with Marlow, who turned back and winked at her again.

Nessa rolled her eyes.

"What was that all about?" Ailes asked when it finally appeared they were alone. He took a drink of his cola.

"Nothing. Marlow just wanted me to have sex with you tonight."

Ailes spit out his drink and looked at her. "And what did you say?"

"Nothing. You aren't my type." Nessa handed Ailes a few bills.

"What is this for?"

"To pay for my drinks."

Ailes handed it back to her. "Keep it. I paid for the night's drinks."

Nessa nodded and pocketed the cash. "You're not upset, are you?"

"About me not being your type?" Ailes shook his head. "Don't worry; I have thick skin."

Liar! Bullshit!

He ignored his brain that was now teaming up with his cock.

"Well, I best be going. Thanks for the invite. You sing well." Nessa stood, turned on her heels, and then left the club.

Ailes took a long draw off his cola, stood, and then walked up to the bar where Brylan was volunteering for the evening since one of the staff had called out. Ailes owned half the club and Brylan owned the other half. Brylan was the brains behind the outfit.

"Got rejected?" Brylan asked as he wiped down the bar.

Ailes narrowed his eyes at him.

"Sorry, I couldn't help overhear it. I know we promised not to eavesdrop on each other, but I thought it would be humorous."

"Asshole," Ailes snipped then asked, "What happened on the corner?" He pointed to a pile of mess on the left side of the bar, and Brylan's face paled. It was vomit. Brylan hated vomit above all else. "You're cleaning that up, and I'm going home."

"Fuck you, Ailes!" Brylan called out to him as Ailes stood and walked out. But before he did, he heard Brylan gagging as he began the cleanup. He deserved it.

~~*~*

Mike watched Marlow as he left the apartment above Hellish. He then followed the man a little way into a parking garage and entered the elevator with him.

Marlow smiled at him. "Kind of cool today, huh?"

"Yes, unusually cool," Mike answered. He put out his hand for Marlow to shake. "My name is Mike."

Marlow took his hand. "Marlow."

Mike smiled and let Marlow walk out of the elevator. He followed close behind him to his car, and before Marlow could insert his key into it, Mike slammed his head into the car door.

~~*~*

Marlow awoke hours later, his head pounding. He tried to move, but his arms were tied above his head. Marlow looked up and saw the giant hook that he hung from. He screamed and tried to escape to no avail.

"Tsk, tsk, tsk. Don't you know, the more you move, the more you bleed?" a voice said in front of him.

"Who are you?" Marlow asked. "Let me go please."

"Let you go? What would be the fun in that?" growled the voice.

Marlow whimpered and tried to free himself. When he failed, he began to cry.

"Aw, poor little human so weak that he can't even protect himself."

"Who are you?" Marlow cried.

Mike stepped out of the shadows, but his face was now a skull with one iridescent blue eye and a socket where his other eye had been. Then Mike smiled, showing rows of serrated yellow and red teeth.

Marlow screamed, and Mike threw back his head, laughing.

Mike walked up to him and brought one hand up to Marlow's face, snapping his head hard to the right and exposing his neck.

"No, please, no. Let me go. Please. I won't tell, I promise," Marlow pleaded, but his request went unheard as Mike brought his teeth down into his neck and bit down.

Marlow screamed, and Mike relished the pain that the man felt. He could feel Marlow's fear and the soul that was nestled within the man. Mike took a sip of it and felt its immediate warmth fill his body. Then Mike backed away, his face covered in Marlow's blood.

He grabbed Marlow by the hair and snapped his head up to face him. "You shouldn't have touched what didn't belong to you."

"What are you talking about? Please just let me go."

"You know what I'm talking about!" Mike growled. "My woman,

you touched her!"

"I'm gay," Marlow said weakly. "I have a boyfriend."

Mike laughed. "You liar. I saw you dance with Nessa."

Marlow looked at Mike. "N-Nessa?"

Mike growled, "You're not allowed to say that name!" He slammed his fist hard enough into Marlow's face that his head and body whipped back violently.

Chapter 11

A iles stared at Nessa's door. He couldn't believe he actually wanted to see her again.

Brylan had told him to leave Nessa alone and stay out of the way, let the Nightingales take care of her, but he, too, was a Nightingale, and he could protect his woman more than they could.

Ailes raised his hand to knock on the door, but it opened before he could, and Nessa appeared, staring at him.

"Ailes, what are you doing here?"

"I wanted to ask if you wanted to take a walk with me." He wasn't sure if Nessa even trusted him. He knew she said he wasn't her type, but he called bullshit on that one, especially after the way she had acted on Halloween night.

Nessa stared at Ailes, not quite sure if what he had just said was a figment of her imagination or not. "You want me to walk with you where?"

Billy stared hard at Ailes from behind her, making him very uncomfortable. It was odd that Billy had that effect on him, since he had known the old man for years and had never given so much as a blush in the old man's direction.

Ailes shrugged. "Maybe down the Royal Mile to Edinburgh Castle."

"*Edinburgh Castle*," Nessa mouthed then frowned slightly.

"Go with him," Billy told her.

Ailes put his hands in his pockets and tried not to show Nessa how incredibly uncomfortable he was at the moment. He had already asked her out once.

Ailes scowled and clenched his fists, and then he looked at Nessa, hoping that she wouldn't agree to walk with him so he could get away from Billy's uncomfortable gaze.

"Or we can just walk to Samuel's apartment," said Ailes.

Don't know when to keep your mouth shut?

"Fine, let's go on a walk."

Ailes did a double take and blinked a few times. "So, you will really go on a walk with me?"

"Don't act so stupid, Ailes. You asked me, and I accepted."

It was a long and silent walk, and the couple barely even looked at each other, which was fine with Ailes. Talking was for those who had something to say.

"You're the singer of a band?" Nessa asked, finally breaking the awkward silence between them. "When were you going to tell me?"

Ailes smirked. "Didn't think you would care what my job was."

"I would've liked to know. You probably could've had an easier time asking me out that night."

"Is that right?" Ailes quipped.

"Yeah, it's not every day you meet a man whose primary job is to sing," Nessa said. "You do something that other people find hard to do for a living."

Ailes pursed his lips. "I didn't say that being a singer was my only job."

"Oh? Then what is your main job?"

"Well, I'm a stripper," Ailes said, trying to keep a straight face.

Nessa stopped walking and stared at him, her wild imagination trying to picture the man standing in front of her dancing and taking off his clothes in front of other women. She was surprised to find she was actually jealous.

Ailes' laughter, deep and smooth as silk, brought her attention back to him.

Ailes was bent over in genuine laughter, which she had never heard until now. What was strange about it all was that Ailes had just tricked her. Nessa didn't know how she felt about that. Should she laugh, too?

"Why is that funny?" Nessa finally had to ask, not getting the joke.

Ailes stared at her for a good long moment and smiled. "I thought I could get you to laugh, Nessa. There isn't enough laughter in the world."

Nessa looked at him, she had never before heard him talk like that. Most times, Ailes was rude and silent, all broody and sexy. What had changed?

"Yes, the world does need more laughter in it," Nessa said.

Ailes smiled at her. "Just like you should have a good time out instead of being stuck at the tattoo parlor or your apartment all the time."

Nessa frowned. "I happen to love my job. So what if I don't go out? What business is that of yours?"

"I just thought you should have more fun," Ailes said.

"What I do in my spare time is my business, not yours. Why do you keep asking me out? Are you doing it as some sick joke?"

Ailes scowled. "No, I'm not doing it as a sick joke. I am interested in being friends with you, Nessa, and friends spend time together. Why in the hell does that bother you so much?"

"Because I don't trust you!" Nessa screamed, her voice loud enough that some tourists turned to look at them.

"If you don't trust me so much, then why do you keep going out with me?"

Nessa shook her head.

"Oh, I see. You go out with me because you don't want to hurt my feelings. Well, here's a news flash for you, Nessa: my feelings aren't easily hurt. But yours, yours is a sense of pride, and that pride causes you to be bitter and stuck-up," Ailes spat

Nessa clenched her jaw and fists. "I should never have come with you."

Ailes laughed. "And there you go, feeling sorry for yourself. Go back to your apartment where you can be alone and miserable."

Nessa shook her head again and tried not to let Ailes see how much his words cut deeply into her. "You're an asshole," she told him then ran before she showed him how weak she truly was.

Ailes crossed his arms and stared at the tourists around him. Then he sighed and rolled his eyes before he ran to catch up with Nessa. He found her in front of a phone booth.

Ailes grabbed her by the arm and forced her to face him. She fought, trying to free herself, but Ailes pulled her into his arms and held her tightly. "I'm a jerk. Just a stupid jerk," Ailes whispered in her ear.

Nessa pulled away and looked at him. "You're actually an asshole."

Ailes smiled. "So that's what I am." He thought for a moment. "You have the most wonderful blue eyes."

"Do I?" Nessa asked, feeling her throat go dry.

Ailes nodded. "Yes, you do, my sweet."

Nessa blushed then stepped away from him. "Let's go."

"Where?"

"To Samuel's apartment. I am curious about how he and Marlow are doing," Nessa said.

Ailes nodded, and then they walked down the Royal Mile.

Minutes later, they walked into the alleyway next to Hellish where they found Samuel.

"How have you and Marlow been?" Nessa asked as she and Ailes caught Samuel on his way to the dumpster with a bag of garbage.

He looked at the couple with a big smile on his handsome face. "Oh, it's going great. I'm so happy. Meagan gets along with him, too." Samuel threw the bag into the dumpster.

They walked with him up into the apartment as they talked.

Chapter 12

Mike smiled as Marlow woke up the next morning. He walked up to him, his cell phone in hand. "Looks like your boy toy has been trying to call you all morning. Too bad he won't be able to talk to you." Mike threw the phone onto the floor, shattering it.

Marlow whimpered and hung his head. He had no strength to move, no hope as his kidnapper stood before him, laughing.

Mike grabbed his hair and forced Marlow to look at him. He gave him that wicked smile full of those serrated teeth that he had felt bite into his skin so many times now.

"Do you want to leave, Marlow?" Mike asked.

Marlow found the courage to lift his head up to look at Mike. *Will he really let me go?*

Marlow's heart soared with hope, hope that he would see the man he had come to love, hope that he would finally get to know the daughter he hoped to one day be a father figure to and walk her down the aisle at her wedding like a father should, looking proud as he and Samuel gave her away.

Mike untied him, and Marlow fell to the floor. He looked at Mike as he stood on wobbly legs.

"Go. You are free," Mike told him, sweeping out one of his arms toward the exit of the warehouse that they were in.

Marlow began to walk slowly toward the exit. He felt so weak and dizzy from the blood loss, but he still continued, the need to be with his love spurring him on.

Marlow opened the exit, stepped outside into the night, and then smiled. He was free. He could go to Samuel, be with his love, and leave this whole thing with Mike behind him.

He heard laughter behind him, around him, beside him.

Marlow tried to run, but still the laughter followed, now with the sound of running footsteps. He tried to pump his tired legs, but they just wouldn't move fast enough.

Marlow saw the gate before him, seeming to become closer to him, promising freedom and his dreams.

He would never make it.

Chapter 13

The next morning, Ailes' cell phone buzzed with a text from Brylan.

Found a body, dead on scene. Blunt force from something stronger than human. Maybe demon.

Ailes frowned as he flung his phone onto his bed and pulled the covers over his head. Brylan was just trying to pull him onto a case so he had a Nightingale on his side to find a murderous demon.

His phone buzzed again, and Ailes grabbed it, frustrated. Instead of a text from Brylan, though, it was Nessa.

Need you. Samuel's boyfriend found dead. Samuel being interviewed by cops. Come ASAP.

Ailes quickly climbed out of bed and dressed. He was out the door and in his car in five seconds flat.

Nessa ran into Ailes' arms when he entered Samuel's apartment. He had never before seen the woman act like this. Usually, she was tough and stubborn as hell. Whatever happened to Marlow had her shaken up really bad.

"He was torn to shreds, Ailes," Nessa whispered. "It's him. He killed Marlow."

Ailes frowned. *Mike? Why?*

Ailes looked at a shaking Samuel, who was talking to Brylan. He pushed Nessa out at arm's length and told her, "Stay here." Then he walked over to Brylan and Samuel.

He grabbed Brylan and pulled him into the extra bedroom. "What leads do you have?"

Brylan shook his head. "Not many. They are interviewing Samuel and Nessa. Eyewitnesses placed them dancing with the victim at the bar the other night."

Ailes growled. "That victim has a name. It's Marlow."

Brylan raised his eyebrows. "You knew him?"

"I didn't know him that well." Ailes snorted, crossing his arms. "And don't think you can pull me in on this. I don't work for the Department of Paranormal Affairs and Investigations."

"Whatever," Brylan said. "This Marlow, he was torn to shreds. Body parts everywhere. No human could have done it. Not unless there was somehow demon blood involved, or it had to be an incredibly strong human."

"It was Mike," Ailes said.

Brylan frowned. "Why would Mike kill Marlow? He had nothing to do with all that."

"I don't know," Ailes said. "Listen, I'm going to take Nessa to Isla's house. If Mike did kill Marlow, then he still plans to come after her."

"That's not a good idea. He might come after you, as well, and follow you to Isla's. You'd just be endangering her. Take her to the Nightingales, Ailes. You know she will be safe there."

"I can take care of her. I am a Nightingale, remember?"

To be a Nightingale meant that you protected those who needed to be protected. That was the basis of the organization. When a mate was found, that mate was automatically protected within the organization. The Nightingales were ancient and had been a part of the world even when the first of the paranormals came to existence. It was an honor to protect your mate and to die trying.

"That's not what is worrying me. Nessa doesn't know demons exist. She only knows that an incredibly strong man attacked her and is now stalking her because she kicked his ass."

Ailes growled, "She will be safe with me. Now drop it."

As Ailes left Brylan alone in the spare bedroom, the detective stared after his friend.

~~*~*

Lariska found her brother Lenarska on top of a rooftop, staring down at two men and a woman who were leaving an apartment surrounded by police.

"She is right there, the human who destroyed my face."

"The elder requests your presence," Lariska said.

Lenarska looked at his sister, his face covered in blood, and smiled.

An hour later, they stood before the elder, who peered down at Mike as a king would a lowly peasant, a sneer stamped permanently on his face.

"We pride ourselves on the anonymity of our clan, Lenarska, who calls himself Mike. You have deliberately disobeyed this edict. Now the humans and likely other demons know of our clan because of your foolishness," Elder Kainez said.

Mike sneered as Elder Kainez continued.

"Thus comes my ruling. You are to excuse yourself to the nest and leave the human girl. You seem too obsessed with her. If you disobey this edict, Lenarska, you will be handed to Lariska, who will then decide your fate." Elder Kainez held out his hand for Mike to kiss. "It is done."

Mike kissed the elder's hand, leaving a small amount of Marlow's blood on it, and then backed away. "If that is your wish, Elder."

~~*~*

Mike slammed into his warehouse and grabbed the nearest woman by the hair. He dragged her, kicking and screaming, into the next room and growled at any of the women who tried to help her. Then he slammed the door behind him.

The other women huddled close together as the unfortunate woman's cries of pain filled the air around them. No one would get

78

sleep that night. No one.

Chapter 14

Nessa tried to help Samuel as he got ready to attend Marlow's funeral. Meagan sat nearby, fixing her hair and trying not to look worried about her dad. It was a sad day for Hellish Tattoo Parlor and for the people who had known Marlow. Even Billy was upset that one of his tattoo artists had lost someone he had loved.

Billy had closed the parlor for the funeral. It was only right. Marlow's murder had been personal, and Samuel had become family.

You didn't mess with family.

Nessa adjusted Samuel's tie and gave him a soft smile, but Samuel just looked at the photo of him and Marlow at the bar with her and Ailes. Marlow and Samuel looked so happy being in each other's arms. It was the only picture that Marlow, and Ailes, for that matter, had allowed to be taken.

Nessa hugged her friend and wiped his tears like a mother would her child.

"It's time, Samuel," Billy said as he came into the room. "His parents and siblings are here."

Meagan walked over to her dad and put her hand into his. "Come on, Dad."

The funeral was worse. Marlow's mother fell to her knees before her son's casket and later blamed Samuel for her son's death.

After the funeral, Billy and Meagan escorted Samuel back to the car.

"Are you coming, Nessa?" Meagan asked, and Billy looked over at her.

"No, I think I will walk for a little bit. Clear my head."

Billy looked worried, but Nessa smiled to reassure him.

"Don't worry, Dad; I will take a bus home."

"That's not what I'm worried about, love. There is still a killer loose out there, and it's not safe to be out alone at night."

"If that killer even gets close to me, he won't have a chance to touch me," Nessa said. It was true, with Ailes following her, she doubted the killer would even get close enough before Ailes got in the way.

"Just be careful, Nessa," Billy said.

Nessa smiled. "Don't worry, Dad. I can call Ailes if I need him." She walked down the sidewalk, away from them and the funeral.

"That's what I'm worried about," Billy said as he got into the car.

~~*~*

Nessa put her hands in her pockets as she walked. She pictured Ailes singing on stage, naked from the waist up. What would his tight abs feel like against her hands?

She shook her head. It wasn't the time to think about that. Actually, it wasn't the time to think about Ailes like that ever.

Nessa heard laughter behind her, which sent chills down her spine and made the hair on her neck stand on end. She turned around but found no one behind her. Hunching her shoulders against the chill of late of fall, she prepared to cross the street when she suddenly found herself being flung onto the street, a snarl sounding close to her ear and the smell of death burning her nose.

A dark man with long dreadlocks, wearing a vest and tight leather pants, came to her rescue, pulling her to her feet and looking around for the man who had just been there.

"Oi, you all right, lass?" he asked.

Nessa nodded.

He looked around again then lead her into a bar. "Jimmy, get the boss! I think he will want to see this."

A skinny man tuning his guitar nodded then disappeared into the back.

Nessa looked at the man and tried to back away from him, but the booth he sat her down on prevented her from going any farther.

The man called Boss walked out of the back, his dark hair covering his face from view. He froze when he saw Nessa and flipped his hair from his face. His eyes were a bright iridescent yellow, his face scarred from his chin to one eye and to his left ear. He was big and burly with muscles and tattoos from his neck down, disappearing into his trousers.

He looked at the man with dreadlocks. "Get the bones," he said as he walked toward Nessa, sat in the booth, and lit a cigarette. "Don't be afraid. No one here will hurt you, not while I am sitting here. No one messes with Boss."

Nessa stared at him, not sure if she should trust this man or his associate. She was in a dark and dingy bar, after all, and the people who were walking around didn't look friendly. She wasn't afraid. No, fear was a sign of weakness, and she wasn't weak.

The dreadlock man came back with "Bones" and she was not shocked to see that Bones was Ailes. Compared to the two men, Ailes looked more compact, muscular, and slimmer.

When Ailes saw Nessa, he pushed Boss aside, grabbed her from the booth, and dragged her to the back of the bar.

"I'm going to borrow the back room, Joe," Ailes called to a heavy-set guy who was tattooing a girl who looked seventeen.

"Take all the time you need, Bones."

Ailes pulled her into the room and locked the door behind him.

"Are you all right?" he asked as he looked her over.

Nessa nodded, still a little shaken. She hugged herself as she walked around the room. "I think Mike attacked me." She showed him the scrapes that she had received when she had been pushed to the asphalt.

"Dammit!" Ailes said.

"I'll be fine," Nessa told him.

Ailes leaned down close to her face, pressing his lips briefly to hers. Nessa stared at him, her breaths coming out heavy, and her heart beating fast.

"I'm sorry," he whispered.

"Don't be." She kissed him back, all her fear and anger going into that kiss.

Ailes broke the kiss. Nessa's lips tingled where his lips had been only a few moments before. Her whole body seemed like it was on fire.

"What is this place?"

"Another bar I own with Brylan. We are equal owners of the bar that you saw me play at and this one," Ailes answered.

"Why do they call you Bones?"

Ailes smiled. He lifted his shirtsleeve and showed her a crossbones tattoo. "Got it on my twenty-first birthday. Was smashed as hell." He lifted his hand and brushed some of her hair behind her ear. "I will be back soon."

He came back a moment later and helped her into a car that he had borrowed. Then he drove her back to her apartment.

"How did your men know to get you? They don't know me."

"Well, I may have told them about you … I talk a lot with them, and things sort of slipped," he answered as he drove.

Nessa couldn't help smiling slightly. He'd talked to his friends about her? Did all men talk about women to their friends?

He pulled in front of the apartment. Nessa looked at Ailes as they climbed the stairs to her front door. The awkward silence seemed to stretch on longer as they stood next to each other.

Nessa unlocked her door and opened her mouth to speak, but Ailes just crossed his arms and frowned slightly.

"Will I see you tomorrow?" Nessa finally asked.

Ailes shrugged. "I don't know. Maybe."

"I hope you are comfortable at Brylan's."

"Nessa, stay with me tonight," Ailes said, shocking her. "Stay with me at Brylan's home. It's being renovated, and he isn't staying at it."

Nessa thought about it for a moment. She would be safer there. Anywhere Ailes was seemed to be safe. Mike wouldn't attack outright if he knew she was with him. It was the logical decision.

She would go, if only for a night, just to get away from the chaos that she seemed to be in.

~~*~*

Mike watched Nessa as she and Ailes walked around her apartment, packing her clothing.

Screw the family and the clan elder. His word was not law here in Edinburgh, and Mike didn't have to follow that law. He wasn't Lenarska any longer, and this wasn't the underworld. If he had to kill a few demons and humans to get his woman, he would. His army would obliterate them all, and that damn half-breed, too.

Chapter 15

Nessa walked into Hellish, feeling a little crappy and angry. She hunched her shoulders and closed her eyes as Mike's torn face and sinister laughter entered her mind.

After Ailes had asked her to come with him to get away from Mike, she had packed her things then left him behind.

Why couldn't he take her dad? Samuel? Megan, too? She couldn't leave them here.

Ailes walked into the parlor a few hours later, and Nessa stared at him. His face told her that he meant business. She couldn't help clenching her jaw and a fist as she thought of what she would say to him.

"You ready to go?" Ailes asked her.

"No, I am not," Nessa responded. "And I never will be."

Ailes growled, "Why the hell not?"

"Can you guarantee Mike won't go after my dad, Meagan, or Sam? Can you guarantee I won't have to worry about Mike finding me there?"

Ailes growled again and moved closer to her. "I cannot promise that."

Nessa shook her head. "You'll just have to force me. I'm not leaving. I can't leave them here while Mike is out for me."

Ailes smirked. "Fine. Then I suppose you wouldn't mind going to dinner with me."

"I don't know. Will my friends and family be invited?"

Ailes smiled, showing a row of perfect white teeth. "Of course."

After dinner, Ailes escorted Nessa back to her apartment while the others had fun talking to each other over leftovers. She had gotten tired of all the small talk, and he had known she would.

Ailes looked at Nessa and leaned against the wall next to her apartment door. "Are you sure I cannot change your mind?"

"Not unless you have a way to keep Mike away from my friends and family," Nessa said, fumbling for her keys.

Ailes clenched his jaw and grabbed Nessa around the neck, putting her in a sleeper hold.

Nessa clawed at his arm and tried to scream, but nothing came out of her mouth. Her vision began to go black, and then she was out like a light.

"I wish I hadn't had to do that," Ailes growled.

Mike had waited for Nessa for over four hours before he realized that she wasn't coming home.

He growled as he broke her window then entered the apartment. He then entered her bedroom and tore apart her dresser and closet. Her clothes were still there, hanging and folded up neatly. He raided her dirty clothes hamper, and the half-demon's smell assaulted his nose.

Mike snarled and tore out every article of clothing until he found the shirt that held Ailes' scent the strongest. Mike tore it to shreds. How dare that filthy half-breed touch her?

Mike grabbed a handful of Nessa's panties then climbed back out the window. He took a big whiff of Nessa's scent and closed his eyes, his mouth turning up as he pictured the fine cloth against her naked skin. He would find her, and she would be his, and the half-breed would pay for ever touching his woman.

Chapter 16

essa's head was pounding, and the person who was speaking to her and nudging her wouldn't stop no matter what she said to stop her mysterious, albeit annoying, assailant. Nessa even slapped at the hand that shook her hard and slapped her face.

Nessa opened her eyes to find an older woman staring down at her. Her lips were thin, and her forehead was crinkled.

"Get up, girl, get up," she said, pulling Nessa into a sitting position then walking around the room. She threw clothes and bedsheets into drawers then turned back around to fetch some more.

"Are you still not up yet?" she asked. "Such a lazy girl. Don't know why he even brought you here."

Nessa stared at her. "I am not lazy."

The older woman put her hands on her hips. "It's past noon, isn't it?"

"*Past noon?*" Nessa mouthed. How long had she slept? Where in the hell was Ailes?

The older woman growled and pulled Nessa out of bed by her arms. "Get dressed and go downstairs, you lazy girl. Chores are needing to be done, and I won't have you lying around." She left, and then Nessa faintly heard Ailes' voice as the door closed behind the woman.

What the hell was that about?

Nessa looked around the room and realized she was naked. She blushed. That woman hadn't said a thing!

She scrambled around the room, seeing no sign of her clothes. *This is ridiculous!* However, Nessa did find a pair of jeans and a T-shirt freshly laundered in the dresser on the far side of the room. She slipped them on. They were a tight fit, but they would do. Nessa then found a brush and combed her hair.

What I wouldn't give for a shower. However, that woman would be back faster than the water could heat up.

Nessa followed the hallway and the smell of bacon and eggs. Her stomach growled. She almost passed the kitchen, but the older woman grabbed her arm and pulled her in.

"Here, girl. Go get milk. Can't have any gravy without it, and he loves gravy."

Nessa frowned.

"I thought I told you to go get milk!"

Nessa looked at the older woman then ducked out of the house as quickly as she could before the woman could whack her in the butt with her broom.

"Lazy despot!" the older woman screamed after her.

Outside, Nessa found a dilapidated barn with a giant hole in its side. It was hardly a place that could hold a goat, much less any other animals.

Nessa walked into it, looked around, and slumped her shoulders. Great, she had listened to a crazy person. There were no animals to be found.

The sound of hammering came from the back of the barn, and Nessa followed it, finding a man standing on a ladder, hammering a new board into place where the giant hole was.

"Hello?"

The man froze and looked at her.

"Detective Brylan?"

"Good morning, Nessa. How did you sleep?"

Nessa frowned at him. "How did I sleep? I suppose I slept great, but what are you doing here and where in the hell am I?"

Brylan climbed down from the ladder and took the bucket from her. "Ah, the old woman told you to fetch some milk."

"Detective, I want to know where I am, and why I'm here."

Brylan held up his hand. "Please be patient, Nessa."

Nessa clenched her fists. "Don't tell me to be patient."

Brylan wiped his forehead then grabbed his drink and took a long draw. "Hey, Ailes! Nessa's awake," he called out. "And the old woman gave her the bucket."

Nessa heard Ailes groan and watched as he climbed down from the top of the barn. He was naked above the waist. His rune and Celtic knot tattoos seemed as if they were playing with each other all over the front of his chest to his arms and around to his back. Nessa stared hard at his chest and counted the tattoos. Then she gazed upon his abs and the happy trail that disappeared beneath his jeans.

Nessa snapped her gaze away and brought her hand up to her mouth, hoping she hadn't been drooling.

Ailes grabbed the bucket from Brylan and put it in the corner of the barn. "There are no animals at all."

"She is getting worse, Ailes," Brylan told him.

Nessa looked at the two men and frowned. "What's wrong with her?"

Ailes looked at her and shook his head as he walked out of the barn.

Brylan sighed. "Isla has Alzheimer's. She thinks she's living on a farm with her husband, daughter, and Ailes. We just go along with gathering milk." Brylan smiled at her. "Well, she sent you out here for a chore, so I guess you should do one. Let's see what Ailes has available for you."

"Wait just a goddamn minute. I am not doing anything until one of you tell me why I am here."

Brylan walked out of the barn, and Nessa followed him.

~~*~*

Clean out the damn coop!

Nessa scrapped poop from the floor. This was ridiculous. She was an artist, not a pooper scooper. How in the hell had she been roped into this?

Nessa scrapped some more poop from the floor and flung it into a bucket she had next to her. Then she sat back on her heels and wiped her face with her arm. How long had she been in here? It was sweltering.

The door of the coop opened behind her, and Nessa turned and saw Ailes looking around

"Wow, you had fifteen minutes and look at this place. Almost free of poop." Ailes looked at her and smiled. "I'm impressed."

"It's not finished yet," Nessa said, standing up and popping her back.

"Well, it looks perfect. Isla will be happy," Ailes countered. "It's time for breakfast. I suppose you would like to eat, right?"

Nessa's stomach growled as she pushed by Ailes and exited the coop. She didn't need to be told twice.

~~*~*

Ailes hammered another board in place then grabbed another from Brylan.

"You're going to have to tell her soon," Brylan told him as he climbed up to the roof and helped him place the board. "The Nightingales will expect her to be knowledgeable about them and the paranormal world and what is to be expected."

"I don't have to tell her anything," Ailes snapped.

Brylan climbed down then back up with another board. "How long do you think you're going to be able to keep the Nightingales from her?"

"She doesn't need to know."

"Right. And you're not worried?"

Ailes looked at him. "No, I am not."

Brylan raised his eyebrows. "Are you saying that you agree with me?"

"And if I did, what are you going to do about it, Detective?"

Brylan stared at him and frowned hard. "I suppose I will have to keep teasing you about it."

Ailes smiled. "I would like to see you try."

~~*~*

Nessa lay down on her bed after dinner that night, exhausted from a long day of working on that damn coop. *Thank God it was done!*

As her eyes grew heavy, Nessa closed them for a brief second before she was shaken awake by a rough hand. She snapped her eyes open and found Isla staring at her with her arms crossed.

Oh God, what does she want now?

"Girl," Isla said, "good job today." The older woman smiled at her then bent over and raised the bucket. Isla put her finger to her pursed lips then left the room.

Nessa lay back down and smiled before she fell asleep for the night.

Chapter 17

The next morning, Nessa was on her hands and knees, cleaning the floors and grout, while the older woman sat at the table next to her, sipping tea as she watched Nessa clean.

"Don't forget to get the corners. Food gets stuck there," Isla said.

Nessa rolled her eyes and continued to scrub. One minutes Isla was praising her, and the next, she was telling her what to do.

"You missed a spot behind you," Isla said, spilling a bit of tea on the floor.

"That's it!" Nessa said, throwing down the scrub brush and standing. "I am done with you.

"Ailes!" Nessa walked out of the kitchen and out to the garage connected to it, where Ailes and Brylan were finishing work on Isla's tractor.

Ailes pushed himself from underneath the large vehicle and looked at her.

"I want to go home. Take me home now," Nessa demanded.

Ailes stared at her as he wiped his face. "You can't go home."

Nessa put her hands on her hips. "Why the hell not?"

Ailes didn't say anything. Instead, he pushed himself back under the tractor.

Nessa pulled him out again. "Tell me why I can't go home."

"Because you're not safe there," Ailes replied, pushing himself back under the tractor.

Nessa pulled him out again. "Ailes, you better tell me why I can't go home."

"I already told you."

She was safer here? She thought back to that night after dinner and it suddenly clicked. Ailes had kidnapped her!

Nessa opened her mouth to bitch him out and tell him what she was going to do to him just as Isla walked into the garage with her purse.

Ailes and Nessa looked at her.

"Ailes, can you take me to Edinburgh today?" Isla asked. "You promised."

"I have to fix this tractor, Isla," Ailes said, looking at Brylan. "Can you take her?"

Brylan nodded then walked over to Isla and grabbed her gently by the arm. "Come on, beautiful."

Nessa stared back at Ailes as he pushed himself back under the tractor. "This isn't over," she told him. "And don't think I don't know what you did."

Ailes banged his head on the tractor. "Fuck!"

Nessa smiled. That would teach him.

She ran out of the garage and to the front of the house to catch up to Brylan and Isla.

"Take me with you," she told Brylan.

Brylan smiled as he helped Isla into the passenger seat. Then he looked at Nessa and offered her a seat.

~~*~*

Brylan walked into the garage and to the tractor that Ailes was still underneath, still trying to fix it.

"I told you; you are not going home," Ailes said.

Brylan laughed. "Oh, that makes me a little sad. I have a great date tonight."

Ailes scowled as he quickly pushed himself out from under the tractor and stood. "Shut up. How's Nessa?"

"She's gone, Ailes."

Ailes walked out of the garage then turned around and looked at him. "What in the hell do you mean *she's gone*?"

"I drove her back home." Brylan laughed. "It was Isla's brilliant plan, and a clever one at that."

"Dammit, Brylan." Ailes ran to the front of the house where his car was parked but found the wheels were gone. "She is not safe in Edinburgh. And weren't you the one who told me to take her to the damn Nightingales?"

"I alerted the Nightingales. They are watching her as we speak. You would do well to do your part and keep within their rules."

Ailes turned and bum-rushed Brylan, tackling him to the ground then colliding his fist with his jaw.

~~*~*

An hour later, Ailes threw his phone onto the table and stared at Brylan, who was icing his jaw and smiling back at him.

"Do you realize what you have done?" Ailes asked.

"Well, I know now that I may have put Nessa into the Nightingales' hands, which you refused to do. For that, I apologize," Brylan said. "I should have asked you about your plan to keep her here to protect her."

Ailes opened then closed his mouth.

Brylan slapped his hand on the table. "Oh, I get it. You're in love with her then?"

"Screw you."

Brylan laughed.

~~*~*

Nessa walked into Hellish just as the parlor opened for the day, seeing Meagan sitting at the reception desk, filling in appointments on the computer.

"Welcome to Hellish. How can I help you?" Meagan asked without looking away from the computer screen.

"Just here to see my dad," Nessa told her.

The young woman's eyes widened at her, and then she quickly jumped down from her stool and pulled Nessa into a giant hug. "Nessa, so glad to see you again."

Nessa pushed her out to arm's length and stared hard at her. "It's great to see you, too." She smiled. "Is my dad in the back?"

When Meagan nodded, Nessa turned, walked through the door to the back, and then entered her dad's workroom. He sat on a stool, tattooing Samuel, who froze when she came in.

"Dammit, Sam, if you keep doing that, you will cause me to give you a bad tattoo," Billy chastised then looked up and stared at Nessa.

He put his tattoo gun down, stood, then walked over to Nessa. "What are you doing here?"

Nessa snorted. "I came to work. I wouldn't miss a day."

Billy shook his head. "You can't be here. You have to go back with Ailes. He said it's the only way to keep Mike from you."

~~*~*

Ailes tried calling Nessa for what seemed like the hundredth time before he threw his phone onto the couch and crossed his arms. She was purposely ignoring him.

Ailes stared into the fire blazing in the fireplace. He had wanted to give Nessa a place where she felt protected, but what did it matter when she wouldn't answer her phone? It wasn't like she was his. At least, not yet.

Ailes closed his eyes and fell deep within himself to that part that he hated and regretted waking up. The thing was cold and unfeeling, and it cared only for itself. It wanted to feed, and the crippling hunger it threw at Ailes was not what he had expected.

He snapped his eyes open and stood, his bones feeling as if they were cracking and his teeth felt sharp.

Freeeeeeeee meeeeee.

Feeeeed meeee.

Ailes shook his head and stumbled toward the door.

Freeeeeeee meeee.

Feeeeeed meeeeeee.

Laughter pierced Ailes' head. He grabbed it and closed his eyes tightly.

Frrreeeeeeeeeee meeeeeeeeeeeee.

Ailes shook his head once more. Finally, his shoulders drooped, and his eyes snapped open to reveal red eyes.

Chapter 18

Nessa pulled up in front of Isla's farmhouse where Ailes was waiting for her. His face was grim, and he didn't look pleased. Nessa got out of the car and stood there, staring at the man who came toward her.

He grabbed her by the arm and pulled her toward the barn. Inside, he slammed the door hard behind her.

"Glad you came back," Ailes said

"What the hell happened to you?" Nessa asked.

Ailes stared at Nessa, not quite sure what she was talking about. He brought his hand up to his face and felt the puckered cuts on his face.

He frowned at Nessa. "Why did you go?"

"Go where?" Nessa asked. "To Edinburgh?"

Ailes growled. "I forbid you from going back there. If you do—"

"What, Ailes?" Nessa walked up to him until they were almost touching. "What would you do?"

Ailes growled as he pushed Nessa up against the coop wall and crushed her lips against his in a kiss of passion and anger. He wanted to take her right then and there, wanted to claim her as his and bury himself within her. She pushed all the right and wrong buttons, and that pissed him off and made him hard as hell.

Ailes broke the kiss and lifted her, and she wrapped her legs around his waist. He moved against the sensitive apex between her legs, showing her just how much she made him want her.

"This is what you do to me, lass," Ailes growled.

Nessa moaned. She couldn't help it. It just escaped her mouth.

Damn, she wanted him right now. In her. Around her. She wanted his cologne on her skin. She wanted his mouth making love to her. She wanted to explode and soar on cloud nine as he moved inside her.

Wait. No.

"Put me down now," Nessa demanded as she tried to push him away.

Ailes gently lowered her to her feet, and Nessa looked at him as she tried to tidy her hair and clothing.

"I can't do this. I have to go."

"Nessa, wait." Ailes tried to grab her arm, but before he could, she was already outside the coop and well on her way toward the house. He should have just well enough alone.

~~*~*

Did that just happen? Did she almost have sex with Ailes? Nessa stared down at the coffee cup that Isla had set in front of her, demanding she drink it because she looked tired. She must have been tired. She had just been in the coop with freaking Ailes! She had kissed him and would have welcomed having sex with him if he had wanted to. Even though it had seemed like the right thing to do, she couldn't have brought herself to do so. Her body almost betrayed her, and she had long ignored what her body wanted.

Nessa took a sip of her coffee, closed her eyes, and moaned. Vanilla and a little cinnamon, just how she liked it.

When she opened her eyes, she found Ailes standing before her, his eyes heavy with lust. Nessa cleared her throat and told her body to shut up.

"Nessa, listen. I—"

"There you are!" Isla yelled, walking from the back of the kitchen and waiving a ladle. "I called you twice, and you ignored me! What's the point of having a damned cell phone if no one answers it?"

98

"I'm sorry. It's my fault. I didn't have it on me, and I should have," Ailes explained.

Nessa lifted her eyebrows. Ailes being amicable? Had that moment in the coop caused him to lose some brain cells?

"That's enough. I am tired of you thinking you can just apologize and everything will be okay!" Isla threw her hands in the air then placed them on her hips. "The downstairs bathroom needs fixing, and the animals need tending, and all you do is lollygag around the house and come to me when you need something. Well, I'm tired of it! You sleep at the mansion tonight."

Ailes opened then closed his mouth, not sure what to say.

"Fine, I will stay in the mansion tonight," Ailes finally said. He looked at Nessa, but she was back to staring at her coffee. He turned on a heel and walked out of the kitchen.

Isla watched him go. She hadn't missed the look that her grandson had given Nessa. Something was going on between the two of them, and she wasn't going to stand by and let it fizzle out.

"As for you!" Isla shouted, wagging her finger at Nessa. "You will pull your weight here. It's the least you can do since I am giving you food and a room to stay in."

"I didn't ask to stay. He made me," Nessa said, pointing to where Ailes had disappeared.

Isla's eye twitched. "You talkin' back to me, girl?"

Nessa shook her head, truly afraid of the small-framed woman.

Isla nodded. "Good. Now go peel potatoes for me. We are having a roast tonight, and you will take some to my idiot grandson."

Nessa looked at her. *"Your grandson?"*

Why hadn't she been told that?

"Yes, now get your patootie out of my kitchen!"

~~*~*

Nessa carried the basket heaped with food and cola through the forest until she came upon the family cemetery, where Isla said her daughter,

Ailes' mother, was buried. Just beyond that was the house called the mansion that had once housed the members of Isla's family until the late 1920s. It was dilapidated now and only a few rooms were livable. Apparently, Ailes regularly stayed there, in a room on the ground floor. Which room, though? Isla hadn't said.

Nessa passed through the cemetery and into the house. It was huge! How could anyone have afforded this?

There was a large chandelier in the foyer where the stairs curved up to the second floor. They were rotted now but still held the cherry red hue that must have been beautiful in the past.

Downstairs housed five guest rooms. Isla had told her that one them led out into a garden and a hedge maze. That one had to be Ailes' room. All she needed to do now was find it.

Nessa searched all the downstairs rooms until she had one left.

She knocked on the door. "Ailes, are you there?"

When no one answered, she pushed open the door and found an empty room. She stood stunned at the breathtaking scene beyond the double glass doors.

Nessa put the basket on the bed and walked over to the windows. What a beautiful garden! Isla hadn't lied when she had said it had stayed beautiful. Damn, they were lucky! She would kill for a view like this. It was a hedge maze, with rose bushes as the hedges and beautiful pottery and statues lining the front of the maze. Nessa noticed a statue of a woman with a beautiful face. She bet it was just as beautiful on the inside as well.

So engrossed with the view, Nessa hadn't realized that Ailes had stepped into the room beside her.

He watched her as the evening sun made her black and red hair look so silky and beautiful. He wanted to spread that hair on a pillow as he took her.

Ailes shook his head. Not the right time.

"What are you doing here?" he asked, making Nessa nearly jump out of her heeled boots. "Sorry, didn't mean to startle you."

Nessa looked him up and down. His hair was wet, and so was his body from the shower he must have just had. He smelled like vanilla and a little bit of man soap. Must have been from his shampoo. It was a pleasant smell.

Most men that she had known, besides Samuel and her dad, had a musky smell from too much body spray. Ailes was different, though. There was no body spray on his beautiful body.

"I brought you dinner." She pointed at the basket. "Don't worry; the big bad wolf didn't have a chance." Nessa went back to looking at the garden as Ailes found a shirt then looked through the basket.

He chuckled. There was a meal for two, a blanket, and some wine from Isla's personal storage. Now he understood what the old woman was trying to do.

Good one, old lady.

He walked over to Nessa, basket in hand. "Let's eat out in the garden." He grabbed her hand, guiding her outside to set up their dinner.

Nessa sat in front of Ailes and took the plate he offered her. Realization struck her as to what Isla had just done.

"She set up a date," Nessa said absentmindedly.

"Yes, she did." Ailes chuckled. "Meddling old woman."

Nessa looked at him. "I didn't know. She just told me that I would be eating soon. I didn't think it would be with you."

"Is that a bad thing?"

"No, just surprising that she would play matchmaker."

Ailes shrugged. "Don't think of it as a date. Let's just have a good time with each other. It's been a while since we did something like this."

"This is only the second time, Ailes. The other times, we were hanging out. This is a date, like it or not." Nessa drank some of her wine. "I will get Isla back for this."

Ailes laughed. "Let's tag team her."

After finishing their meal, Ailes walked her around the garden, and then they both retired to the mansion as the sun set and darkness settled in.

A kitten mewled at her ankles, and Nessa picked it up. "And who is this?"

"That is Thor. He is a food whore," Ailes said.

"What about your band?" she asked, loving on the kitten.

"What about it?"

"You seem to be away too much for it to go on tour."

"Well, right now we are between gigs. And I have something here at home that I want to protect."

Nessa blushed crimson and turned away. She let the kitten go.

"What happened to your mom, Ailes?" she asked, changing the subject.

Ailes sighed and threw a log onto the fire that he had set in the fireplace of the main hall. Thankfully, it was not falling apart like the rest of the house.

"She died when I was twelve." Ailes looked at her. "She left me at home and never came back. After I turned eighteen, I finally found out she had been murdered, and that's when I found Isla and began to live with her. She had been kept from me, but I knew who she was for a long time before I moved in with her. Where is your mom?"

"My mom is not that important to talk about," Nessa said, taking a sip of her eighth glass of wine.

"Hey, no fair. I told you about my mom. It's only fair you tell me about yours."

"Fine. My mom was a wealthy woman. She married my dad when I was a baby, but she never really liked me for some reason. When I turned eleven, she left us. She loved her money more than she loved us. I don't know what happened to her." Nessa downed her wine then lifted it toward Ailes for another glass. Instead, he took it from her and put it on the table.

"Listen, I know I have been an ass lately and not very friend-like.

It's hard for me to make friends because of my attitude and what I am. People freak out and run away before ever taking a chance to see me."

Nessa stared at him. "What you are is a handsome man and an asshole."

"No, Nessa, I am much more than human." Ailes stared into her eyes. "You won't like me after I show you my other half."

His other half? What is he talking about? Is he married? Oh God, I'm alone with a married man!

"What other half? I wasn't aware you were—"

Ailes put a finger to her lips, and Nessa stared down at it. A clawed finger! *What the hell?*

Nessa quickly backed away and watched as Ailes took off his jacket. He sprouted leathery wings! Freaking wings! *What the fuck?* His tattoos glowed all up and down his body as he stood before her, all claws and leathery wings.

Nessa stood slowly and approached Ailes, his red eyes staring straight into her as she stopped in front of him. She raised her hand and touched a wing. Then she slid her hand down his shoulder to one of the glowing tattoos.

"I wouldn't blame you if you ran, Nessa, but I can't guarantee I won't bring you back here kicking and screaming," Ailes warned. "Are you scared?"

"Terrified. But I won't run."

"Why not?"

"Because, this is you. I know you would never hurt me."

He moved closer to her. "No, I won't."

Nessa swallowed. "A rock star and now … I don't even know what to call you."

"We go by many names. Demon, angel, fae. I am a half-blood. But we call ourselves Nightingales."

"Nightingales? What are Nightingales?" Nessa asked breathlessly.

"We are an elite group of demons, half-demons, fairies, and other beings that protect the human race from evil beings. We also are an organization that protects the supernatural world from those who would abuse us," Ailes explained.

"So you're …?"

"I am a half-demon."

"Meaning you have human blood, right?"

Ailes nodded. His woman was smart, very smart.

Nessa brought her hand to his chest. It was warm, very warm. Then she stood on her tip toes, wanting to kiss him, wanting him to consume her. She pressed her lips to his and felt it as Ailes slowly lost the transformation and deepened the kiss.

Nessa moaned as Ailes picked her up then deposited her on the bed, breaking their kiss to stare at her.

"I don't care what you are, Ailes. I just want you right now," Nessa said.

Ailes growled. "Are you sure that isn't the wine talking, lovely?"

Nessa shook her head then pulled off her shirt and bra, freeing her breasts.

"Fuck! You are torturing me, lass." Ailes touched one breast and played with a rosy nipple. Nessa moaned.

He gently pushed her to her back as he took the other breast into his mouth and swirled his tongue around the nipple as he played with the other. Nessa arched her back and let out a cry as the pleasure hit her over and over in a hot mess from her nipples down to the spot between her legs.

Ailes popped her breast from his mouth and gabbed ahold of her jeans, peeling them off. "No underwear?" Ailes chuckled, and Nessa whimpered.

He slid his hands down her beautiful, pale skin and came to stop between her legs. He played with her clit as he leaned down and made love to her with his mouth.

Nessa moved her hips up and down as she felt the pressure build and build, finally crying out her pleasure.

"God, you're beautiful," Ailes told her as he pulled his own shirt and jeans off, dropping them to join her clothing on the floor.

Nessa stared at his cock that was ready for her as Ailes climbed on top of her and kissed her until she was in a dizzying haze.

"Oh please, just take me," she moaned, but it came out as mostly a whimper.

"You must be sure, lass, because, when I take you, you will be mine forever."

"I don't care. Just do it," Nessa said, begging for release.

Ailes entered her in one thrust, and Nessa cried out as yet another wave of pleasure brought her up and over. No man had ever made her feel this way.

He pulled her into another deep kiss then lifted her hips and thrust into her, going as deeply within her as he could. Nessa cried out and exploded over and over, each explosion taking her to a place of absolute pleasure and finally to cloud nine as Ailes growled and plunged as deeply as he could and spilled himself into her. He collapsed next to her on the bed.

Nessa looked at him and said, "I don't care if you're half anything, but don't you dare transform without telling me. I want to have sex with you when you do."

Ailes laughed.

Nessa climbed on top of him and guided him into her with a moan.

"Fine. You have me. Take your time with me, my insatiable lass."

Chapter 19

Nessa awoke to Ailes deep inside her. She let out a cry of pleasure as he spilled himself into her once more then lay next to her on the bed.

"The sun looks nice today. How about a trip to Edinburgh?" he asked as he kissed her shoulder and lips. "We can check in on Samuel and your dad."

As Nessa stretched, the blankets slid down to reveal a rosy nipple. Ailes slid it into his mouth before sliding down to make love to her. Nessa cried out as he again brought her over the threshold then lay back.

Nessa immediately climbed on top of him and slid his cock within her, riding his cock.

Ailes laughed. "You're insatiable."

Nessa moaned as he grabbed her hips and brought her up then hard down on his cock.

"Fuck, lass!" he cried as he spilled within her once again, holding Nessa against his chest. "No more. You've tapped me out."

Nessa laughed. "I thought you could deal with an insatiable lass like me?"

"Only if she gives me a break." Ailes pushed her black and red hair back and kissed her forehead.

~~*~*

An hour later, the couple drove in Isla's car to Edinburgh with a list of things the older woman had demanded they get. One of which kind of made Nessa and Ailes blush in embarrassment when they read it. Condoms.

That brought up another thought that they hadn't thought of, but Nessa assured him that she was on the pill. She needed to pick those up from her house.

After the shopping was done, Ailes drove Nessa to her apartment, where they found it ransacked.

"What the hell?" she uttered.

"Stay here. I'll check it out," Ailes stopped her from going farther into the apartment.

He checked the bedroom, her studio upstairs, and her bathroom. He was on his way back when he saw a man lunge at Nessa, grabbing her by the hair and pulling her hard toward the fire escape. Ailes growled and beat him to it.

"Where do you think you're going with my woman?" he hissed and transformed. His demon blood coursed through his veins, lighting up each tattoo with his magic. Ailes then pulled one of the tattoos from his arm and flung it at the man. This spell stopped the man in place long enough for Ailes to grab Nessa and get her to the safety of the bathroom.

Ailes then walked back into the living room and stood in front of the man. There was a crow tattooed on his forehead, indicating he was a zealot—a human who had sold their soul to be indentured to a demon or vampire family.

"Who is your master?" Ailes demanded, but the man refused to speak. Ailes pulled another tattoo from his arm and brought it before the man. "You know what this is?"

The man began to sweat.

"It will be painful death if you don't tell me who your master is." Ailes brought the misty tattoo closer and closer to him until the man finally broke.

"Mike is my master!" the man blurted. "He made me stay here and wait for Nessa to take her to him. Please don't hurt me. I am only the messenger."

Ailes let the tattoo disappear then pulled out his cell phone and hit speed dial for Brylan. "Now you will be a jailed messenger."

~~*~*

Nessa was not happy with Brylan at the moment. Ailes had wanted to take her to see Billy and Samuel, but Brylan had quickly vetoed it when the messenger—they called him a zealot—told Brylan what he had told Ailes. Deemed "unsafe," Nessa would need to return to Isla's.

"I'm sorry," Ailes told her. "I didn't think Mike would send one of those men after you."

"You said he was a zealot; why?"

Ailes drove into Isla's driveway and parked before he looked at her. "A zealot is a human who has given themselves to a demon or a vampire. They have nothing to lose, because they usually have no families or friends or are told they have none."

"So, not only do demons and half-demons exist but even vampires?"

"Yes, Nessa. Last night was no magic show I put on for you. It was real. Every being you've ever heard about is real."

"Even the fae?"

"Oh yeah. And don't get me started on them."

"Why? Aren't they supposed to be beautiful?" Nessa asked.

"Oh, they are beautiful but conceited and worse assholes than me. They think they rule this world."

He and Nessa climbed out the car and started unloading the groceries for Isla as they continued their conversation.

"The world, unfortunately, is ruled by the seven."

"The seven?"

"There are seven lords, each of them from different paranormal sects. Vampire, werewolf, shifters, demons, fae, and angels."

Isla met them at the door. "You're telling her *now*? *After* what you both did?"

Ailes and Nessa looked at each other then asked at the same time, "Did what?"

"Don't play dumb with me. And get the groceries in here before I get my meat hammer and bludgeon you both to death."

Nessa pursed her lips as she imagined Isla's wiry frame running after the meat hammer.

Ailes put the groceries on the counter. "We were attacked at her apartment, and it was ransacked."

Isla looked Nessa over. "You're not hurt, are you?"

"No, I'm fine."

Isla rounded on Ailes. "This happened because of you and your meddling ways. You get yourself into these situations and don't think how it would hurt me."

"There was a zealot," Ailes continued, ignoring her. "And I was always going to tell her about the seven and more about the Nightingales. She knows about me, Isla, and didn't run from me, so don't you be worrying your pretty little head about her knowing these things."

"I knew it!" Isla clapped her thigh. "Something did happen between you!"

"That's not important right now, Isla. Nessa needs help. And you, Brylan, and I can help her."

Ailes looked at Nessa. "I am an ass, but not one who lets those I care about get hurt."

Chapter 20

*H*e *cares about me?* When had that happened? He was an asshole, or he had been. Was this the true Ailes? Nessa hoped so. She didn't know if she could take it if he was just stringing her along. She knew she was heading down a rabbit hole that would destroy her.

That was three days ago, and in those three days, she had learned about different types of paranormals and creatures who shared their world, and the Nightingales. To say she was still in shock was an understatement.

"Tell us if all of this is too much for you," Isla told Nessa over a cup of coffee.

"Not too much right now. I mean, I just learned that we are not the only ones here on earth, and that there is a group of people who protect people of all types."

Isla nodded. "I felt the same when my daughter told me about it, and then I met her man, Ailes' dad."

"Was he really a demon?"

"Yes. He was handsome, but he loved humans and truly wanted to help us. There wasn't a wicked bone in his body … or so I thought. Everything changed when she died." Isla wiped the tears off her face. "I just know that Ailes' father had her killed. He was a Nightingale. He was also a clan elder within the Oso Demon clan. They are a powerful clan."

"I'm sorry," Nessa told the older woman.

"Don't be. I believe that people make their own choices, and my daughter made hers the day she met Ailes' father and joined the Nightingales."

Nessa drank her coffee and didn't say anything. It was best not to, since Isla was obviously bitter about her only daughter falling in love with a demon.

Even though Ailes' father had been good, it didn't mean that the others were. Ailes had made that perfectly clear three days ago when he and Brylan had educated her about their people.

There were different types of Nightingales—half-breeds and full breeds fae, werewolves, and other types of paranormals. Then there were those who were evil that the Nightingales fought. Those who were evil hid in the shadows, and Brylan and Ailes said they preferred to live in nests. Mike was a demon who lived like that. It explained why he chased, stalked, and taunted her. He was a true demon from the underworld.

Mikalio, Brylan's father, she had learned, was part of a family of Nightingales who held humans in high regards. That meant they protected humans and paranormals from the bad. But they refused to work alongside other beings in the DPAI—Department of Paranormal Affairs and Investigations. Ailes had told her that DPAI was a part of Interpol, a group who was against paranormal rights.

Nessa took another sip of coffee just as Ailes looked at her and smirked. She knew that smirk.

He drained his coffee then walked out of the kitchen.

Nessa thanked Isla for the coffee then ran after Ailes as he was heading into the barn.

Once inside, Ailes pulled her to him, lifted her flowered skirt, and then tore her underwear off.

Nessa pouted. "I loved those."

Ignoring her, Ailes lifted her, and she wrapped her legs around his hips. He entered her in one swift thrust, and Nessa moaned. Still thrusting, Ailes laid her down on the hay and made sweet love to her.

Brylan made his way to the barn to "milk the goat" for Isla and instantly regretted it as he heard the moans coming from the building. He went in to investigate and found Ailes and Nessa buck naked, and Ailes going to town on her.

Brylan pursed his lips and turned on his heels.

Poor Brylan.

~~*~*

Later that night, Nessa and Ailes shared the room in the mansion again, wanting to be far away from Brylan and Isla, who had begun to meddle and ask them personal questions.

"Do you think everyone could live in peace together?" Nessa asked suddenly.

Ailes looked at her. "Probably. We all have our own tiers. The Nightingale full bloods think half-bloods are lower than them, unless you have human blood and have a parent in a Nightingale family who holds an influential part in the family."

"Like a king or queen?"

"Yes, but we call them honorable elders. They are the ones who hold power, because they have lived for a long time. As for Fae, werewolves, vampires, and other paranormal creatures, I suspect they have their own elders and tiers of power. I don't know much about their lives, but Brylan does, since his mother is fae."

"Wow! A fae?"

Ailes nodded.

Nessa snickered. "So, are his wings those little fly wings?"

Ailes laughed. "No, and don't let him hear you say that. He kind of gets upset when people mention his mother. They don't have a great mother/son relationship."

"What about your mother? Isla said she was human. Does that mean she was a woman of power within the Nightingales?"

Ailes nodded. "She was a very important woman. I remember how it was before she died. Life was easy, because she had a lot of influence over my father, Lariat. He would do anything to please her. She had him wrapped around her pinky finger."

"Why did she run?"

"I don't really know," Ailes said, playing with Nessa's nipple. "I guess she'd had enough of Lariat's pride. He was the elder of the family, so he had a lot of sway. I like to think my mother made him jealous because she was easily likeable. That gave her the power to keep him on his toes."

"But he murdered her," Nessa said.

"That's how the story goes. I know what I saw, though. She kissed me and left and never came back." Ailes looked at her. "Lariat's crime is vanity. He loves himself and nothing but himself. When my mother had been alive, he'd loved her. Or, at least I like to think he did. I didn't see love between them, but she shared his bed and birthed him a son and a daughter."

Ailes kissed her on the forehead. "Enough of this depressing talk. You need to sleep."

"But I'm not tired yet," Nessa whined.

Ailes laughed. "Go to sleep, or I will punish you."

"Oh really? How?"

Ailes climbed on top of her and showed her.

Chapter 21

Ailes and Nessa woke to a loud *boom!* They hurriedly dressed and ran toward Isla's home to find it engulfed in flames.

Ailes screamed in anger and began to chase the zealot who just stood there, staring at the flames, while Nessa ran up to the house and found Brylan lying on the ground, bleeding and unconscious.

"Isla!" she cried out, trying to find a way into the burning building.

Nessa heard Isla's screams as she found a door to the basement. She put her hand on the knob and pulled it open. The flames hadn't gotten there yet.

In the corner, stood Isla, and Mike was standing over her.

Nessa growled and rammed into him, knocking him off his feet to crash into the pantry to his right. She then grabbed Isla and pulled her to safety, slamming the basement door shut and propping a large log over it to keep Mike inside. She helped Isla walk to Ailes and Brylan, who was now conscious.

"Mike is here," she told them. "I locked him inside."

Ailes shook his head. "That won't work. He can get out. He is a full demon—flames don't hurt us as much."

The house exploded again, and the four of them stared as the house fell in on itself.

Nessa saw Mike, just as Ailes had said, walking out of the fire unscathed. His zealot was not so lucky. He ran around, engulfed in flames, and then fell quite dead onto the ground as Mike ran toward the forest.

The fire died down an hour later, and the Nightingales had come to collect Brylan and Isla to take them to hospital. There was no saving the house. All the hard work and family memories that Isla had had in that house … gone in a puff smoke.

Nessa looked at Ailes as they followed the ambulances to the hospital. He looked worried and angry, really angry. His fists clenched the steering wheel. She reached over and touched one of those fists.

"Don't touch me!" Ailes snapped at her.

Nessa pulled her hand back. *What the hell is wrong with him? Why is he suddenly upset with me?*

Ailes parked in the parking lot and got out of the vehicle. Nessa followed.

"Ailes, please talk to me."

He turned on his heels. "You want to talk? Well, how about, every time you are with me, something happens! First, my home, and now Isla and Brylan are involved. How many people have to get hurt? I can't do this anymore. I am sorry, but you have to leave. Isla needs me." Ailes left her there in the parking lot

Nessa pushed back the tears and the lump in her throat. Then, in anger, she began to walk from the parking lot and started the long walk back to Edinburgh. It would take forever, but she was so angry that she didn't care.

She finally made it two hours later, walking into Hellish as Samuel and Meagan were closing up.

Meagan ran up to her. "What happened to you?"

"Long story. Can I stay with you tonight?" she asked Samuel, who nodded.

Meagan jumped up and down. "We'll make it a girls' night. I can't wait!"

Nessa forced a smile. Yeah, a girls' night. She would let the younger woman believe that.

Chapter 22

iles was happy to know that Isla would be okay, but he wasn't so sure about Brylan. The man was tough, but now DPAI had him on suspension due to the Nightingales' presence and was doing an investigation into why Mike had a zealot burn down Isla's home.

The demon was obsessed with Nessa, and Ailes was powerless to stop it.

He looked around the lobby for Nessa. She wasn't there, and he wasn't shocked. He had been an ass to her and had taken all his anger out on her for what Mike had done.

Ailes saw Brylan sitting in the corner, his head in his hands. He walked over and sat next to him.

"How bad is it?" Brylan asked. "Did Mike hurt her?"

"No, just some smoke inhalation and a few burns. They are keeping her overnight just in case. What about you?"

Brylan looked at Ailes. "Could be better. Lost my job with DPAI."

"What! I thought you'd be on suspension at the least?"

"Yeah, they thought about that and said, since I didn't catch the zealot and Mike, I wasn't fit for DPAI. I couldn't even protect Isla or Nessa if I wanted to."

"What are you going to do now?"

"Other than keep my detective license? Nothing. I am through with DPAI. Tired of their rules and favoritism toward others in the unit. You fuck up, you're gone." Brylan sighed. "Besides, Mikalio offered me a position with the Nightingales. They need someone to train the new members."

Ailes nodded. "You make a better detective with the Nightingales than special agent with DPAI anyway."

Ailes then sighed. "I drove Nessa away tonight. Told her that it was her fault the house burned down and Isla was hurt."

"Don't worry; Nessa is smart. She will come around … Maybe."

"Asshole."

~~*~*

"So, he just left you alone with a maniac running around Edinburgh?" Meagan asked. "What is he? An asshole?"

Nessa chuckled. "Yes, and I was a fool for sleeping with him."

Samuel gave her a cold cola. "Everyone makes mistakes. At least you learned before the going got tough."

Meagan looked at her dad and scowled. "It's not like he just dumped her, Dad. He got mad at her. I imagine that he was just worried about his grandma. I would be if Grandma Betty had been in the same situation."

Samuel snorted. "Your grandma would have bit Mike. And Ailes is not right for you, Nessa; believe me. I have been down that road, and Billy would agree."

"No, he won't, because he will never know I slept with Ailes, or that we were even together." Nessa took a drink of her cola. "Besides, I am a grown woman, and I can date whoever I choose, even if they are assholes."

Meagan stared into her drink. "At least he didn't leave you for your problems like mine did."

"You had a boyfriend?" Samuel and Nessa asked at the same time.

"Sure, I did. I am a grown woman. I have needs, too."

Chapter 23

Ailes found Nessa at Hellish, tattooing a client. Good to know she could return to work and forget about his attitude and him completely.

He walked up the desk where a cute young woman sat typing away on the computer.

"Ugh! Stupid machine!" She banged on it with her hand.

"You can hit it all you want, but it won't make it listen," he told her, and she looked at him. "I haven't seen you here before. My name is Ailes."

The young woman narrowed her eyes, stood, came around the counter, and punched him as hard as she could.

"Meagan!" Nessa yelled, throwing down her tattoo gun and coming out of her workroom. "We don't hit the cust—Oh, it's you." She turned back to Meagan. "If you can, take the bat my dad has and hit him in the balls." Nessa walked back into her workroom and went back to working on her client.

Ailes stared at the petite woman before him. She wasn't letting him out of her sight, her eyes following him.

"Do I need to move you?" he asked her as Billy came out of the back.

"Ah, just the man I want to see. Come on back here, Ailes, so I can show you my new tattoo design. I think you might want it when you see it."

Ailes smiled at Meagan. "Seems I am welcome here after all. Try to keep your temper to a minimum. It's not ladylike."

He followed Billy into the back and sat down in the chair that Billy used to tattoo his clients.

Billy brought out a sheet of paper and handed it to him. "What do you think?"

~~*~*

When Nessa finished with her client, she walked up to the front where Meagan was banging on the computer again. "We really need to get a new computer," she told Meagan.

Meagan looked at her and gave a sad smile. "Billy said it's perfectly fine and we don't need another." She nodded at the glass counter where tape held the glass together. "He won't even replace the damn desk."

"I will talk to him; see if he can let me replace those. It's ridiculous not to have a working computer or desk for our finest secretary."

Meagan beamed.

Ailes walked out from the back with Billy, his arm bandaged. When he saw Nessa, he patted Billy on his shoulder, paid him, and then walked over to her.

"We need to talk."

"Do we? Because I'm sure that the last time we talked, you told me that it was my fault that Isla's house is gone."

"I know," Ailes said. "Let's talk outside please … away from the young and older spectators."

Nessa looked around and saw her dad, Samuel, and Meagan watching them closely.

"You're right; let's discuss this outside."

They walked away from the building as Meagan, Samuel, and Billy stepped out of the parlor, still watching them.

"What's going on with them?" Nessa and Ailes heard Billy ask Samuel.

"It's better Nessa explains to you what's going on," Samuel said.

Billy wouldn't find out anything about her and Ailes, not if she could help it. She would talk to Ailes then walk away from him. Fears aside, she didn't need him. Not for protection and definitely not to save her like she was a damsel in distress.

"Listen, I know I was an asshole, and I shouldn't have blamed you for Isla getting hurt or her home burning. It's not your fault that Mike did this. You could no more help him stalking you than you could help that he burned down the house," Ailes explained.

"Damn right it isn't my fault!" Nessa screamed and poked him in the middle of the chest. "And I don't need some man to come and tell me how it's my fault because you think that your life is pitiful because I am being stalked and bringing Mike into your life. *You* said I would be safe. And until a few days ago, I didn't even know he was a demon!"

Ailes nodded. "I know, Nessa, and I apologize for that. Please come with me to see Isla. She is asking for you."

Nessa wiped the tears of frustration from her face. "Is she all right?"

"Just some smoke inhalation and burns on her left arm. She is a strong bat and will pull through well enough. I wouldn't be shocked if she's out soon with all the ruckus she is making."

When Nessa sighed, Ailes gave her a puppy dog look. She never thought he could make such a cute face with him being serious all the time.

"Stop!" she told him. "Fine, I will go. Just let me close my workspace."

~~*~*

Isla was her usual self—crotchety and demanding. She even demanded Nessa and Ailes to take her home, and when Ailes reminded her that he was having to fix up the mansion to live in, she got angry. That was when the nurse told them it would be best to leave and come back when Isla was in a better mood.

Ailes drove them to Isla's to comb through whatever was left of the smoldering aftermath. Brylan had beat them there and had managed to find photos, pots and pans, and some of Isla's wine storage that had escaped the flames luckily enough.

"How is she?" Brylan asked Nessa and Ailes. "Never mind. I don't need to ask. I bet she is giving everyone a hard time." Brylan showed them the bag and its contents that he had managed to save. "At least she will have some of her sentimental things at the mansion."

"How is construction?" Ailes asked.

"Going. Ellas has them building as fast as they can. They already got a room done for Isla, and you already have that one done for you and Nessa to share." Brylan looked at Nessa. "Unless you want a room of your own."

Nessa shook her head. "I'm good with sharing with Ailes. I just want to make sure Isla is comfortable. Is there anything I can do to help?"

Ailes opened his mouth to tell her it wasn't necessary when a feminine voice beat him to it.

"You can help us set up Isla's room." A woman walked up to them and took Nessa's hand. "I am Ellas, Ailes' sister. I am sure he told you about me."

Nessa looked at him. "No, he hasn't."

Ailes looked back at her and mouthed, "*Meant to.*"

Ellas pulled Nessa along with her. "Come. Let us talk about the room for Isla. It needs another woman's touch."

Ellas was Ailes' half-sister and princess of the Oso demon clan. She shared the same mother and told Nessa that, as the eldest, she'd had to watch over Ailes and raised him. In a way, Ellas was like Ailes' mother. Ellas had long, flowing black hair, unblemished pale skin, and curves that went for miles. She was tall and slender and held her head high with confidence. That had to be the princess in her. She was a nice woman and helped Nessa organize the room to Isla's liking.

Nessa could tell that Ellas loved her grandmother as much as Ailes did and would do anything for Isla.

Chapter 24

Ailes watched Nessa as she helped Isla in her garden. It had been three weeks since the house had burned down and they had moved into the mansion.

Ailes wrestled with the decision on whether he should tell Nessa that he loved her. He had never done it before and had on many occasions told her he cared about her a lot, just as he cared about Isla.

Ailes rubbed his face. It seemed all too complicated—this love thing.

Ailes walked out of the house and toward the small garden, carrying two glasses of tea and handing them to the women.

"This is so good, isn't it? A garden, sunshine, and thanking God that I am no longer in the hospital."

"So you keep saying." Nessa snorted. "You never shut up about it."

Isla laughed. "I do it because there were no handsome men as my nurse. I would have killed for a Mr. Dreamy."

Nessa and Ailes looked at each other, and then helped her up to her feet.

"I think I will go make a cake. It's the right day for a cake," Isla said, shuffling back toward the house.

Ailes squatted down next to Nessa. "How are you doing?"

Nessa looked at him. "Fine. Just feel a little more tired than normal. I think it must be the calm and the fact that Mike hasn't been seen or heard from, which is strange."

"Yes, I have to admit he has been strangely silent these last three weeks. Maybe he decided not to stalk you anymore."

Nessa shook her head. "I don't think he would do that. You've seen how obsessed he is with me."

Ailes nodded and helped her up to her feet. "Maybe you need to nap. You have been working too hard these last three weeks."

"Yes, I think I will. If Isla comes back out, can you help her plant the pansies? She really loves them." With that said, Nessa walked up to the house and disappeared inside.

Ailes watched her until she was out of sight then kicked the shovel. *Why can't you tell her you love her? So stupid!*

Nessa lay down on the bed that she shared with Ailes and started to close her eyes when she suddenly felt sick to her stomach.

She stood and ran to the bathroom, vomiting violently until there was nothing left. Then she sat back against the wall and pushed her hair from her face.

When she eventually stood, she jumped, finding Isla in the bathroom doorway, staring at her.

"Got a stomach illness, girl?" Isla asked.

"I guess so, haven't been holding anything down."

"Are you pregnant?" Isla exclaimed.

"No!"

"Hmph. Well, only one way to find that one out. If you're carrying, we'll know soon enough," Isla said.

"No, that's not necessary … I don't know," Nessa said, not sure what to do as panic set in.

Her birth control pills! She had never grabbed them after all the chaos with the zealot break-in.

She wasn't ready. Oh God, she wasn't ready to be a momma.

"I will get you a test when Brylan takes me to Edinburgh."

"That's not necessary," Nessa said then immediately had to run back into the bathroom to throw up while Isla held her hair back. "On second thought, get one. I need to know, but I am sure this is food poisoning or something else."

~~*~*

Nessa shook her head as they stared at the stick that slowly turned to positive.

Isla looked at her. "Three tests, girl. You're pregnant."

Three tests. All of them positive. Freaking positive!

Nessa shook her head again. "Must be a false positive. I'm going to see my doctor in Edinburgh."

Isla threw the tests into the trash bin. "Do what you want, girl, but I know you're pregnant. You might want to tell Ailes."

"Not yet."

~~*~*

An hour later, she sat in a doctor's office, with Meagan sitting next to her.

"I never been called to sit in on an appointment before," she told Nessa

"You're only here to pinch me if the doctor comes in and tells me I'm pregnant."

Meagan snorted. "Ailes will likely be an ass about this, you know?"

"I don't care what Ailes is going to think. My body, my rules."

Meagan looked at her. "You're not going to do anything to the baby, are you?"

Nessa shook her head. "I may not be ready to be a mom, but I would never hurt the baby just because I don't want one."

"Good. My momma did that. Her boyfriend got her pregnant, and the next thing I know, she comes home and wasn't preggers anymore."

"Meagan?"

"Yeah?"

"You're not helping."

Nessa walked out of the office in a zombie-like trance. It was true, as Isla had said. She was pregnant, about three weeks along. How was she going to tell Ailes? Her dad? Or even Samuel? She had made Meagan promise not to say anything at all about the results. She barely knew the other woman, yet she had a feeling she could keep a secret.

"Nessa," Meagan called to her, fear in her voice.

Nessa looked at Meagan, and then she saw him. Mike was standing across from them, and this time, he was alone with a gun in his hand.

"Meagan, run. Don't look back."

"Nessa, I am not leaving you."

"RUN!"

Meagan took off, and Mike pulled the trigger, hitting Meagan in the back. As she fell to the ground, Nessa jumped on Mike and began to wrestle the gun from him.

He shot again, and Nessa flinched as the shot deafened her.

She watched as Meagan tried to flip open her phone while being beaten by Mike. Nessa tried to scream but heard nothing and was helpless against Mike's strong arms as he leapt onto her.

Soon, she saw a car pull up and watched as Brylan ran up to Mike and jumped him.

Sound returned to Nessa in a rush. She ran over to Meagan, who lay unconscious on the ground. This was all her fault. If she hadn't had her come with her, then Mike wouldn't have attacked her.

Brylan came over and scooped Meagan into his arms while telling Nessa to drive to hospital.

It had all happened so fast.

Mike screamed and chased after them as Nessa drove. He leapt onto buildings and landed in front of the vehicle. Nessa hesitated only for a second before she pressed her foot down harder on the accelerator.

Mike's face elongated as a high-pitched scream filled the air, blowing out the windows. He then leapt into the air, and Nessa kept driving, glancing in the rearview mirror to find Mike being mowed down by another vehicle. She only stopped when they pulled up to the emergency room door.

The nurses came out and rushed Meagan into the back and to surgery.

Ailes, Samuel, and her dad found her pacing in the waiting room half an hour later.

"I am so sorry, Samuel. I had her go with me. I am so sorry." Nessa cried for the first time since her mother had left her.

Samuel grabbed Nessa and hugged her tightly. "It's not your fault," he whispered over and over again.

Ailes grabbed her when the surgeon came out and told them that Meagan had made it out of surgery and was recovering in ICU. Samuel immediately went back to see his daughter.

"What happened?" Ailes asked her.

"I went to see my doctor, and I wasn't paying attention, and Mike attacked us."

"Wait. Why were you at the doctors?"

Nessa shook her head. "I don't want to talk about it right now."

Nessa told Ailes about the gun, about Brylan coming to their rescue, and that Meagan had been shot in the back and beaten while she had been helpless.

Ailes clenched his fists. He wanted to storm out the hospital right then, find Mike, and kill him for touching his woman. *How had Brylan known to be there? Was he tailing them for the Nightingales?*

Billy grabbed his daughter and told Ailes it was high time she rest after being through so much. Ailes agreed, but that wouldn't stop him from hunting Mike.

Ailes found Brylan at the vending machines.

"How did you know about the girls? Are you tailing them or did another Nightingale tip you off?"

"Nope, just doing my job as a detective. Had a case up that way—

dead prostitute. Saw the girls and Mike and decided to intervene. Of course, they would have been okay if you had gone with them."

"I wasn't aware that they were even going to the doctor. How could I have known?" Ailes covered his face with his hands.

"Listen, it's not your fault. I am just angry about my case. They are okay. That's all that matters."

Chapter 25

Finally far away from Ailes, Nessa stared long enough to examine the yellow police tape blocking her dad's door before she dug her apartment key out from the plant next to her door, unlocked it, and then went inside her apartment.

Two weeks had passed since Meagan had been shot. Since then, her dad had been taken to the Nightingales' compound after Mike had done some damage to his apartment.

Nessa closed the door behind her and walked around her apartment. Nothing was the same, and it wasn't homey like Isla's had been.

Nessa went through her closet, looking for anything that she could use as a weapon, and found the Winchester knife that her dad had gotten her when she had begun working nights at Hellish.

She took off her right boot and tried to find someplace she could hide the knife. She pulled off the other boot then ran back to her room and came back with a pair of combat boots that she had modified with canceled pockets that she could use when she went hiking with her dad. She hid the knife in one of the pockets then put them on.

Nessa then armed herself with a steak knife, hiding it in the pocket of a leather jacket that she had put on. When she was satisfied, she left.

She walked down the street, noticing humanoid shadows following her from all sides. She swallowed hard and kept walking as Hellish's neon sign came into view and, with that, a tall man standing in the road.

As Nessa got closer, she saw he was holding a cigar and could smell its strong scent.

The man smiled at her. "Good evening, Nessa McRae."

~~*~*

"When did she leave?" Brylan asked Ailes. "Are you sure she isn't coming back?"

Ailes looked at him. "I don't know. I need to find her. Mike could be anywhere."

"Get off your ass and go after her then."

Ailes laughed. "You are horrible at pep talks. Besides, I don't know where she even went."

"Well, I didn't want to say it, but I think, at this moment, we need help," Brylan said. He pulled out his cell phone.

Ailes stood. "Don't you dare call that bastard. He will use Nessa. He will make her part of his mercenaries. There is nothing he won't have her do for him, even smuggle drugs into the city."

"What other options do you have, Ailes?" Brylan asked. "Mikalio is the eyes and ears of the Nightingales. Unless you want to hunt Nessa, and I doubt her trail is still fresh by now."

Ailes rubbed his face and growled. "Fine, call him, but he isn't to touch her, and he only gives me the information. I will find her."

Chapter 26

Nessa followed Ellas into a dining room where Lariat and Mikalio sat separately with others around giant tables. There were a few tables with other people and young children eating and talking with one another, like they were one, big family. And there, right by Mikalio, was her dad.

Nessa felt a lump in her throat forming, but she quickly stamped it down. If she showed any sign of weakness, Lariat would use that against her. She had been warned about that.

Her dad smiled at her, and Nessa gave him a brief nod as she passed.

"We will be sitting beside Mikalio. His table is opposite of my father's," Ellas explained.

"Why?" Nessa asked as the hungry eyes of Lariat's table followed them as they made their way to the chairs beside Mikalio.

"You are under Mikalio's protection until Mike comes for you. We will try to protect you after that. Any who wish to attack will have to fight Mikalio." Ellas gave her a smile. "And we are the opposing side to Lariat's leadership."

"Ellas, I don't think you should smile about that," Nessa said when they were seated.

Ellas laughed but covered it with a sip of her wine.

Nessa looked back at Lariat and the members at his table, at the heated gaze he gave his daughter.

This is going to be fun, Nessa thought, taking a huge gulp of her own wine.

Mikalio turned toward Nessa. "Watch your back. The demons at that table will make any excuse to attack you."

Nessa looked at him, but he refused to meet her gaze.

"I am a friend, Nessa. And because of my influence within this family and the demons with human lovers and the children of the Nightingales who have agreed to protect you, don't do anything stupid that will make them regret their decision. And don't make me regret my own, or I will allow those demons to have you."

"Are you threatening me?" Nessa asked, squeezing her knife handle.

Mikalio laughed. "Girl, you'd know if I was threatening you. No, it is a promise."

~~*~*

"Well?" Ailes asked for the third time that night. To say he wasn't worried about Nessa would be a big lie. With Mike after her, he had every reason to be.

"She's at the Nightingales' compound," Brylan said, rubbing his eyes.

Ailes balled his hands into fists and tried not to leave the room in a rage. He knew that it was wise to come up with a plan, and he knew that the Nightingales would protect Nessa from Lariat and Mike for now. They would fight until their lives ended.

"I suggest we wait go to the big house," Brylan said, staring at his phone. "Mike will come for her there, Lariat will see to that. The Nightingales can only do so much, I am afraid," Brylan added, noticing the look on Ailes' face.

Ailes sighed. She would be safe with the Nightingales for the moment. He just had to remember that. He hoped they could get there in time before Mike did and Lariat made his deal. His father was against the Nightingales and only thought of whatever deal would bring him benefits. Even if those benefits didn't benefit the clan.

~~*~*

133

Mike plumped the pillow on the bed that he had made for Nessa. Then he looked around. The whole room had been made up for her.

A tattooing chair was in one corner of the room, and a huge walk-in closet in the other. There was also a small kitchen and living room set. His queen would feel at home, and he would make her happy, so very happy. She would forget that half-breed, and then he would die.

Lariat was giving him a great gift, and the Nightingales couldn't do anything about it. They would be helpless in Lariat's house. After all, the Nightingales couldn't interfere with a leader of Seven.

Chapter 27

Nessa didn't dare question Mikalio, or even mention what he had told Nessa in the dining room. what he had told her had clearly been for her ears only. Somehow, however, Ellas had to know what Mikalio had told her. The woman seemed smart and seemed to know everything, or nearly everything.

She looked around Ellas' room. It was huge, big enough to fit at least more than two people. It wasn't surprising since the big house was a renovated warehouse close to the sea. That meant that Mike wasn't living too far, as the warehouses in this neighborhood seemed to house demons and their families.

Nessa plopped down onto her bed and turned her head toward the nightstand. She frowned. The drawer was partially open, and she swore there was what looked like a tattoo gun inside.

Nessa sat up and opened the drawer, pulling out a necklace with a miniature tattoo gun now connected to a long, thick chain.

"Mikalio had that made for you when he found out that you were with Ailes," Elias said.

Nessa dropped the necklace onto the bed.

"I hope it's not too much."

Nessa stared at it then burst into tears. If it hadn't been for her tattoo gun, she never would have had to be here in the first place. And yet, she was moved by Mikalio's gift and grateful for that gun for saving her life and cursing her. She never would have known Ailes was her love.

"You don't like it?" Ellas asked, walking over to Nessa and sitting next to her on the bed.

"No, it's nice. I just didn't expect to receive a gift from Mikalio," Nessa explained, putting on the necklace.

"Mikalio says it symbolizes your courage and strength." Ellas pulled out a necklace with a clear blue heart that had a smaller, purple maze in the middle. "Mine means love, hope, and guidance."

"Does Ailes have one?"

Ellas nodded. "His are his tattoos and a ring that belonged to our mother."

"He never told me what his tattoos mean."

"He never does. Mikalio did some of them himself when he was younger, and Ailes dislikes him for that. He believes it robbed him of his childhood—whatever childhood he could've had without our mother," Ellas explained. "It's best if Ailes tells you that part of his story."

"If I ever see him again," Nessa said.

"You will. You just need a little push," Ellas said, standing then walking out of the room, leaving Nessa sitting there, confused at the woman's vague remark.

~~*~*

Ailes and Brylan stood by the gate, waiting for Mikalio, keeping a constant lookout for Lariat's men or Mike.

Ailes looked at Brylan. "Let's just go in. We can find Nessa on our own. We don't need Mikalio."

"Is that so?" Mikalio said as he walked out from a door on the side of the building. "You never were one to follow the rules or listen to good advice."

Ailes snorted, crossing his arms. "If you didn't take so long getting here, I wouldn't consider going in without you. Not that I need you anyway. I am a Nightingale, remember?"

Mikalio opened his mouth to scold the younger man, but then Brylan cursed, looking around the corner of the building as a car door slammed shut.

Mikalio and Ailes followed Brylan's gaze and watched Mike walk to the gate.

"Damn, I was told that he wasn't scheduled to show up until Monday," Mikalio said. "Damn you, Lariat. Hopefully, Ellas has been told of his arrival and got Nessa out of there."

"If you would have just let us go in and get my woman, Ellas wouldn't have had to get Nessa out."

~~*~*

Ellas froze on her way to her bedroom to turn in for the night. Mike was sitting at the table with her father.

She began to make her way quickly back to her room, but before she could get to it, she saw another demon that she knew walking with Nessa, who was in handcuffs.

When Nessa saw Ellas, she began to fight the demon and was immediately punched in the stomach.

"That is not necessary," Ellas said, helping Nessa before she could fall to the ground. "Who gave you permission to retrieve Nessa from my room?"

The other demon growled, "Lariat told me to."

"You better expect that I will be discussing your treatment of Nessa with Mike."

The demon sneered, "Disgusting human."

"I will be taking Nessa to Mike. You go back to the hole you crawled from."

The demon quickly left, happily.

"Thanks," Nessa said once she got her breath back.

"Don't thank me just yet. We still have to get you out of here," Ellas told her.

Ellas pulled her along down the hallway in the opposite direction then they had been heading. They walked a ways and into a living room, where they stopped in front of the fireplace. Ellas then uncuffed Nessa and pulled on a statue on the mantel, causing the back of the fireplace to slide open.

"Go. Follow the tunnel until you get to a door at the end. Go through it and don't look back," Ellas instructed. "And don't worry about me or Mike. I'll handle everything."

Closing the fireplace after Nessa had gone through, Ellas then walked to the room where her father and Mike were sitting.

Lariat stood, staring at her hard. "Where is Nessa?" he asked, walking around the table and to his daughter. "WHERE IS SHE!" he yelled, but Ellas refused to flinch and remained motionless.

Mike scooted his chair back and walked up to Lariat, standing behind him. "If Nessa is not here, then you are no longer of use to me."

Lariat growled and tried to turn around but found he couldn't move.

Ellas' face looked horrified and, Lariat knew, as his knees began to give out, that he was dead.

~~*~*

Ailes, Mikalio, and Brylan walked into the sitting room and into the blood bath.

Mikalio ran to Ellas, who was lying next to a very dead Lariat.

"What the hell happened here?" Brylan asked then wanted to immediately rescind the dumb question when Ellas and Ailes said, "Mike."

~~*~*

"Why in the hell would she send Nessa this way of all places?" Ailes grumbled as they walked down the tunnel behind the fireplace.

"Her heart was in the right place," Brylan tried to assure Ailes.

Ailes snorted. "She's endangered not just Nessa but Isla now, too. Don't think Mike won't come for her once he knows she's taken up residence at the old mansion."

"Let's hope she understands that she must not interfere, no matter what she sees," Brylan said.

~~*~*

Nessa knew where she was just as she stepped out from the tunnel—the hedge maze behind the old family mansion.

"Nessa," she heard Mike say, and then hysterical laughter followed. "Come on; we haven't got all night."

Nessa ran, unsure how far the hedge maze twisted and turned, or where Mike was or how far away. She only cared about putting enough ground between her and the dangerous demon.

~~*~*

Mike followed the scent of her perfume, figuring out which direction he should go. Soon, the wind blew in the wrong direction, and he was left to track her. So, he waited. Waited for her to make a sound, a mistake that would give him direction. She would be his, no matter what.

Chapter 28

Nessa found herself at a dead end. A fountain that had seen better days stood in the middle of part of the hedge maze.

She cursed, looking around. There would be no secret door to take her away from here. She would have to go back the way she had come and risk running right into Mike. What choice did she have at this point? She should stay and fight, stop running, and stand her ground. Either way, she would probably end up dead or Mike's trophy to show off when he pleased.

Nessa swallowed as she heard Mike's breathless laughter behind her. She turned to face him and her fate, preparing herself to fight.

"Isn't that just great? My one and only is going to fight me," Mike said. "I knew there was something I loved about you."

"I'm not yours, and I never will be. And if you think you will change my mind, you'll have to kill me," Nessa told him, puffing out her chest and looking the crazed demon in the eye.

"After I'm through with you, you will be begging for me," Mike growled, running toward her.

Nessa was caught off guard as she was grabbed by her neck and brought in for a forced kiss. She fought back and managed to find Mike's groin, kicking as hard as she could. Mike threw her into the fountain, howling with rage.

"You want to play rough, Nessa?" Mike growled.

Nessa tried to pull herself up, but before she could, Mike grabbed her by the hair and dragged her from the fountain and through the maze. Nessa screamed in pain and tried everything to break free, but every movement made Mike tighten his grasp on her hair.

Nessa screamed again, this time as loud as she could, hoping that the shrillness of it would make him stop and let her go. When Mike did stop, she knew it wasn't her scream that had done the trick, though.

She heard the familiar *click* of a gun and looked up.

"Daddy," Nessa sobbed when she saw her dad standing there, holding a gun and pointing it at Mike.

"You let my daughter go, you freak!" Billy pulled the trigger.

~~*~*

"Was that a gun?" Brylan asked.

Ailes ran toward the sound, with Brylan close behind.

Please don't be dead, Ailes prayed.

They rounded a corner and was met by a woman, who smiled at them as she raised a gun. Her stomach was rounded with pregnancy.

"I won't let you interfere with his wishes," she said.

"Ronnie?" Ailes asked.

"Don't call me that. Only my man can call me that!" she screamed.

Brylan stepped around Ailes to stand between them. "Go get Nessa. I'll handle this."

Ailes didn't question Brylan, running past Ronnie. Her human speed was no match for his, but that didn't stop the woman from trying to shoot him.

Brylan grabbed her and managed to wrestle the gun from her, throwing it away from them. What was with this woman?

"Let me go! He will kill you for touching me!" Ronnie screamed.

Brylan slapped her across the face, and Ronnie stopped moving, looking at him in shock.

"You slapped me," she stated, her lower lip trembling.

"You tried to kill him," said a male voice behind them, and Brylan turned to find Samuel standing there, holding Ronnie's gun. "Raise your hands in the air."

Brylan was shocked when Ronnie complied.

He looked back at Samuel. "What are you doing here?"

"Billy called me; said Nessa might be in danger, and then I saw her"—he indicated Ronnie—"follow you inside. Billy said Nessa would be here, and so would the man who attacked her. He overheard it and some guy named Mikalio."

"And you hoped you could help her?"

"Well, Billy is, so I can, too," was all Samuel said, and Brylan couldn't help laughing. The old woman had found a way to sneak around after being told not to interfere.

"Wait. Billy is here?"

~~*~*

Ailes found them in the old courtyard part of the hedge maze, in front of the old fountain. Mike held Nessa by the hair and was bleeding from a gunshot wound.

"Well, if it isn't the half-breed," Mike commented. "Come to save your woman?"

"And kill you," Ailes added.

Mike laughed and lifted Nessa up, forcing another kiss, and then he put his face into the crook of her neck and took a huge bite out of her shoulder. Nessa screamed, and Mike laughed before throwing her into the fountain.

Ailes roared and ran toward him, allowing his demon side to take control as he crashed into Mike, fists flying.

Billy ran to his daughter and helped her out of the fountain and onto the ground. He pulled his shirt over his head and tried to staunch the blood flowing from the huge wound on her shoulder as he watched Ailes and Mike fight, not sure what to make of what he had thought were two normal human men. *What the fuck is going on?*

Ailes grabbed Mike and threw him into a hedge bush. The demon crashed through it and onto the ground beyond. Ailes then ran to Billy and Nessa, looking her over before looking at Billy.

"Get her out of here," he told him. "There's an exit to the right. Keep left and don't stop."

Billy nodded, and then Ailes helped him pick Nessa up and walked them toward the exit, away from the old courtyard.

"Stay to the left," Ailes reminded the older man then went his own way in search of Mike.

~~*~*

Billy carried his daughter, following the directions Ailes had given him, but then he was stopped in his tracks by a cruel laugh.

"Sweet daddy loving his little girl," Mike's voice taunted him maliciously.

Billy lifted his gun and cocked it, but before he could take a shot, Mike jumped from atop a hedge and crashed into the father and his daughter.

Billy's gun slid across the ground as Mike took his head and smashed it into the ground. Billy saw a flash of stars as his head connected with the ground.

He tried to fight back, thinking, *This is not how I'm going to die. Not at the hands of this freak!*

Just as Billy started losing consciousness, Mike was grabbed and thrown off Billy by an enraged Brylan.

"You son of a bitch!" the detective shouted as he threw the demon. "Think you can attack innocent people in my presence? You have another thing coming."

Samuel ran to Nessa and Billy as the clouds opened up and rain began to fall. "Don't worry; help is on the way."

Samuel watched Mike and Brylan fight. In the flash of lightning, when Mike looked at Brylan, Samuel could have sworn that his handsome face turned into a face that didn't look so human. It looked like a skull with a sunken face with a socket where an eye should have been. He didn't know what to make of it.

Samuel focused his attention back on Billy and Nessa, trying to make them as comfortable as possible. He looked at the unconscious pregnant woman a few feet away and checked her to make sure she was still breathing. Then he took off his jacket and went back to Billy. He waded the jacket up and put Billy's head on it. Then he stripped off his shirt and tore it into pieces, wrapping Nessa's arm and shoulder.

Samuel had just grabbed his gun when Ailes stepped around the corner.

"Where is that coward?" Ailes asked him.

Samuel pointed in the direction Mike and Brylan had run.

Ailes took off, and Samuel guessed he had found what he was looking for because he didn't come back.

~~*~*

Mike punched Brylan and knocked him unconscious. Then he turned just as Ailes crashed into him.

Mike growled and bit his arm. Ailes screamed and pushed Mike away.

"Never said I didn't fight dirty," Mike said.

"Neither did I," Ailes growled.

Another shot from a gun cracked through the air, and the two turned to find Billy, a gun pointed straight at them.

"You shouldn't be here. Where is Nessa?" Ailes asked.

"She's fine, no thanks to you freaks!" Billy said, the gun shaking in his hand.

"Please put the gun down, Billy, and go back to Nessa," Ailes said, a little taken aback that the older man would call him a freak.

"Don't tell me what to do. I should kill you right here," Billy told him.

"Fine, but you should kill the man who attacked Nessa first." Ailes looked at Mike, but he was nowhere to be found. When he looked back at Billy, he found two Billys wrestling for the gun.

Ailes growled and stood. "You coward! You would make yourself into this man instead of face me?"

Both Billys stopped fighting and looked at him.

"What's going on?" both of them asked.

Ailes shook his head. "You disgust me. We are not playing this game!" He attacked them both and knocked them to the ground.

A demon couldn't make himself look exactly like the person he was copying, and Ailes knew Billy had a tattoo on his right hand with Nessa's name on it. He looked at one of the Billys and found what he was looking for. He lashed out, taking the gun from him and shot him.

Billy looked up at him, confusion on his face, as he brought his hand to his chest. That's when Ailes realized his mistake.

He looked at the other Billy as he transformed back into Mike and was already running and laughing. Ailes pulled the trigger again and hit his mark, injuring the demon. Then he turned back to Billy.

"I'm sorry," Ailes told him, tears that he couldn't stop ran down his cheeks to mingle with the rain and blood. "Please don't die. Nessa needs you. I am so sorry."

Billy shook his head.

Ailes gathered the older man in his arms and carried him toward the exit. "You're going to be okay. Just hang on. I will get you some help."

Ailes walked for quite a way, not realizing that he was out of the hedge maze and that Billy was quite dead in his arms.

"I'll get you help. Please don't die. I'm sorry," he said over and over as he walked.

Ailes slipped in the mud and fell to his knees, still holding Billy tightly.

"Ailes," he heard Isla's soft voice beside him as she knelt down. "Brylan and Mikalio want to take Billy now. You don't have to carry him anymore."

Ailes looked at her. Brylan, Mikalio, and Samuel were standing beside her. When had he gotten out of the maze?

Mikalio bent down and gathered Billy from Ailes' arms.

Ailes watched as his oldest friend was carried away from him, limp and unmoving. He clenched his fists and began to punch the ground and scream.

"Go to Nessa, Ailes. She needs you," Isla said.

Ailes stood and took Nessa's limp form into his arms, carrying her away, just as Mikalio carried Billy away from them forever in the opposite direction.

Chapter 29

Ailes hung his head into his hands and tried to drown out the image of Billy's dead eyes staring at him, his soul no longer within his body. He looked at his hands. There was a lot of blood on them and not all of it was Billy's. When had he begun to care about the blood, about his reputation, about the human woman lying in a coma before him, and her father? When? And, from what the doctors had said, she was pregnant. Why hadn't she told him? Was he not a good mate to her?

Ailes looked up as Brylan walked into the room with the nurse and motioned for him to follow. Once out of the room, Brylan brought out a manila envelope and handed it to him.

"What is this?" Ailes asked.

"Billy left it in case something happened to him," Brylan told him. "Hellish goes to Nessa and you."

Ailes looked at Brylan and blinked a few times. "What?"

"I know it's hard to believe right now, but Billy explains in his last will and testament that he trusted you and, as his friend, he wanted Nessa and you to have the parlor."

Ailes shook his head. "I don't want the parlor. It's Nessa's and always will be. Billy was wrong about me. I wasn't his friend. I was his murderer." He nodded toward Nessa's room. "She will see that soon, as well."

Brylan watched Ailes walk back into Nessa's room and slide the glass door closed.

He snorted. Ailes was allowing Billy's death to get to him more than it should have. Ailes hadn't let anyone's death get to him before, yet now he seemed like a man who had just realized that he actually cared and allowed himself to grieve.

It's about time, Brylan thought, turning on his heels and leaving the hospital.

~~*~*

That night, Samuel woke up Ailes.

Ailes stared at the man then quickly looked to where Nessa's bed had been and jumped to his feet.

"Where is she?" he demanded, walking toward the glass door to find a nurse.

"Stop!" Samuel demanded. "They took her for a CT scan. She will be back in an hour. Sit down and calm down before someone decides to throw you out." He sat himself down on the couch. "They should, seeing as you're not even acting guardian or family."

Ailes looked at him. "She's mine, and I am as good as her family. I've known her father for years. What about you? You've only known her a few months. And what about your own daughter?"

Samuel refused to look at him. "Meagan is fine for now. Go get some rest."

Ailes walked out of the room, brushing past Brylan as the man entered the room he had just left.

Brylan looked at the spot where Nessa's bed had been, but instead of the panic that Ailes had exhibited earlier, he simply shrugged and placed a vase of flowers on the counter.

"They don't allow those in ICU," Samuel said.

Brylan looked at him. "They aren't for Nessa," he said. "For all they know, they are for Meagan."

~~*~*

Ailes walked through the double gates of Hellish. Inside stood four men combing the scene and logging all the items.

148

"May I ask why you are here?" Ailes asked.

All four men stopped cold in their tracks and turned to look at him at the same time with a hiss.

Ailes stepped toward them. "Don't make me ask again."

The man closest to Ailes gave him a toothy smile. "We mean no harm, dear elder. We were called here."

"Don't call me that. I am not an elder," Ailes growled. "Who sent you here?"

"Mikalio. He told us that you would need our help," said one of the other men who seemed to walk on air.

Of course, Ailes noted, *wraiths*. No wonder they were all in sync. They were one entity.

"Stop with the crap, wraith, and return to your true form. And you can tell Mikalio that I don't need anyone's help."

The wraith pulled all its forms within itself then followed Ailes around the parlor.

"Listen, Elder Ailes, you know I don't like Mikalio. He is a pompous ass and is only out for himself. And I personally hated Lariat, but Mikalio sent me here to help you because of *her*," the wraith explained.

Ailes let the old moniker slide, his interest piqued. "Because of who?"

The wraith gingerly walked to the back of the parlor and into Nessa's workroom.

When Ailes stepped inside, he froze. What he saw at that moment was Nessa's soul lying back on the chair, seemingly asleep.

He tried to pass the wraith, but an unseen force pushed him back.

"Tried that already," the wraith said with a chuckle, pointing toward a man in a black pinstripe suit and hat, standing in the corner of her workroom, picking his nails with a knife. "He refused to let me through."

Ailes narrowed his eyes then realized he was staring at Antoine, a friend from his childhood who had left to become a guardian of humans in a place he could not go.

Ailes rubbed his eyes, frustrated. No wonder the wraith couldn't get in. It had to be a being who was divine, or had more power, or near the same power of the divine who could enter the barrier.

Ailes lifted his arm and rolled back his sleeve. He looked at the rune that was inked into his skin and sighed. Then he took a deep breath and, with his other hand, ripped the tattoo from his skin while muttering an age-old incantation. The tattoo floated in the air until Ailes removed a piece of paper from his pocket and enclosed it inside. Then he folded it and pocketed it. This would allow him to pass the veil unscathed.

"That's disgusting," the wraith said.

Ailes looked at him. "Seriously? You find *that* disgusting?"

The wraith raised an eyebrow. "You ripped the tattoo from your skin. Magic or not, that is disgusting."

"So is eating the dead," Ailes told him just as he passed through the wall of protective magic and made his way to the guardian standing in the corner.

"I always knew you were different, Ailes; just didn't think you were on the other team," Antoine said.

"I'm not on any team. Besides, the last time I checked, there were no teams."

"According to her kind, there are." Antoine nodded toward Nessa's sleeping form.

"Humans are imaginative. They create things, and then sometimes manifest things that are not good for them. We are not the manifestations of a feeble human imagination," Ailes explained.

"What about Nessa?"

"What about her?"

"Does she not have one of those feeble imaginations?"

"No, Nessa is better than that," Ailes said. "She is more like a muse who inspires people."

"Or a demi-goddess," Antoine said matter-of-factly.

Ailes simply looked at him.

"She is strong. Unnaturally so," Antoine explained. "And because her soul sleeps here, I was sent to protect and watch over her." He smiled. "She is very important, and we wouldn't have known just how much if Mike hadn't attacked her or she had met you."

"She is not a demi-goddess. You are wrong. Her father was a normal human."

Antoine was shaking his head before Ailes could say anything else. "I've had the honor of reading Billy's will. He leaves this parlor, the apartment complex, and all his worldly possessions and money to Nessa, his daughter whom he adopted from the Lady Hera Orphanage." Antoine smiled again. "An orphanage that existed only long enough to send out beings of divine and fantastical abilities to be adopted by humans, normal humans of no special abilities."

Ailes frowned and looked at Nessa. "No wonder she was able to take Mike's hits and not die instantly."

A demi-goddess. What did that mean for Nessa now? What did it mean for their relationship? It was taboo for a demi-goddess and a half-demon to be together, but not impossible. Would she even want anything to do with him when she found out she wasn't who she always believed she was? Anger could overtake her, and then maybe she would leave.

"Incredible. Even now, she fights Mike. The wounds he inflicted on her are poisonous," Antoine said then looked at Ailes. "There is love here, with her right now; some from her friends, some from Billy, and then her love for you. I don't understand why a demi-goddess would be attracted to a half-demon elder, but to each their own." Antoine laughed. "I can't wait to see the old people cringe. It's a new day and age, and they want it to stay in the old ages."

"What will happen to her?" Ailes asked, changing the subject so the guardian couldn't see just how much learning that Nessa loved him affected him.

"Soon she will wake up and will most likely freak. They all usually do. Don't worry, though; Nessa likely won't die." Antoine looked at Ailes then distanced himself from the half-demon.

Chapter 30

Brylan pulled up to a warehouse and parked his car next to a cop car. He climbed out and made his way to the cop. Now that he was working for himself, he could work the case freely without limitations.

"What's going on here?" Brylan asked, flashing his badge.

"Thanks for responding, Detective Brylan. We got a call that some workers down at the docks heard yelling coming from this warehouse."

"Did you contact the owner?" Brylan asked.

"No owner listed."

Both men turned toward the building when they heard a woman's voice calling for help.

Brylan frowned and pulled out his gun. "Cover me."

Brylan followed the cries to the side of the warehouse and found two double doors padlocked. He turned to the officer. "I need something to break that. Do you have a bolt cutter?"

The officer shook his head.

Shit!

Brylan closed his eyes, holstered his gun, and grabbed the chain. Then he looked at the officer and said, "Don't freak out." He yanked the chain from the door.

The officer's eyes went wide, and he looked almost as if they would fall from their sockets, but as suddenly as it came, it went just as fast.

The girl cried out again, and Brylan ran into the building, his backup keeping a safe distance back. Everyone did that; it was human nature.

He was half-fae and held power that could be felt by those around him. It was a curse and a blessing. It had helped him with Mike, and now it helped him here.

They followed the cries to a room deep within the warehouse and found another padlocked door. *Seriously!* Some higher divinity was seriously cursing him right now.

He looked at the officer and found that he was looking the other way. Using this to his advantage, Brylan pulled the padlock from the door then kicked it in and ran into a room full of screaming, pregnant women.

~~*~*

Ailes hadn't wanted to leave Nessa, but she was in good hands with Antoine. The guardian would watch over her until she woke up and guided her so that he could talk to her.

He was afraid of her leaving him, making the choice to move on and not look back. It had happened with his mother, and that had nearly killed him. He had only been a boy then and hadn't understood what death really meant, or that there was an afterlife.

Antoine had told him that his mother would make a choice, and it most likely would be him, as no mother would choose to abandon their young child.

Boy, had Antoine been wrong.

What if Nessa chose to go to the afterlife with her father and relatives? It would kill him far worse than his mother leaving him. He couldn't guarantee that he wouldn't go after her and pull her back to him.

Ailes looked at the text from Brylan that had pulled him away from his love.

Found women, pregnant. All claim to be married to Mike.

That was not a good sign.

~~*~*

Ailes parked the car beside Brylan's in front of the warehouse and tried to keep his anger and shock under wraps when he saw the women, all in varying stages of pregnancy. He climbed out of the car and made his way to Brylan.

"How many?" he asked.

Brylan's lips thinned. "At least thirty, and one of them just died." He nodded toward a body bag. "They were calling for help, because she had just given birth. They didn't know what to do, and the poor girl died before we got here." Brylan sighed and rubbed the back of his neck. "I need you to identify her."

Ailes looked at him and scowled. "I don't know any of these women."

"I think you do, Ailes. The woman who died is Ronnie."

Ailes flinched as an image of Ronnie's beautiful, laughing face flashed in his mind. She had been taken to the hospital but had checked herself out. No one knew where she had gone.

He nodded then followed Brylan toward the body bag.

The medical examiner looked at the two men, asking for permission. Ailes nodded, and then the M.E. unzipped the bag.

There lay Ronnie, pale cheeks and beautiful face sunken in, and her hair was a matted mess.

"It's Ronnie," Ailes said, and then the medical examiner zipped the woman back up.

Ailes looked at his friend. "Where is the baby?"

Brylan nodded toward the ambulance. "She is going to be okay. Was born healthy and will be taken into the big house."

Ailes shook his head. "Good. We cannot allow the child to be fostered."

Brylan looked at the medical examiner, who pretended to lose his pen and sent his assistant for another. He nodded at Brylan and Ailes to continue talking.

"She is not a human. If she is Mike's daughter, then she is a half-demon and will need to be put with her own kind."

"I agree, but where would we put her? The women will already need to be sent to shelters, and what about their babies?"

Ailes pursed his lips. His grandmother was going to kill me for this, but he didn't see any other choice. "Take them to the family home behind Isla's. The Nightingales are there. If anything, they can find husbands within and help to rebuild the old place. They will be safe and not have to worry about human eyes judging them."

Brylan chuckled. "Isla is really going to kill you for that one, and so is Mikalio, but I will do as you say. You are our leader now, whether you like it or not."

Ailes growled and would have punched the detective, but his phone beeped, signaling a text from Antoine. He pulled it out.

Nessa is awake. Be quick. I have held her off from meeting her relatives. They are pissed, and the wraith has been knocked unconscious.

"I have to go," Ailes told Brylan. "Nessa needs me."

Chapter 31

Back at Hellish, Nessa was again trying to break Antoine's barrier.

"I told you already; you can't leave this room," Antoine said for the tenth time. He was tempted to go back on his promise to Ailes and just let the damn woman go. She was a handful and strong to boot.

He looked at the poor wraith lying unconscious on the floor next to where he stood. *Poor bastard.*

"If you would just tell me what was going on, I wouldn't try to leave. But you keep me here and don't tell me anything!" Nessa screamed at him.

Antoine smiled. "I already told you what you need to know for now. My name is Antoine, and I am your guardian. You cannot leave until you have met the prerequisites, and right now, one of those prerequisites is late as hell. Now calm your ass down and sit."

Nessa screamed in frustration but did as she was told. "All this talk of prerequisites sounds like I am in university again."

Antoine nodded. "It's sort of like that, just without the endless booze and sex."

Nessa looked at him, wondering if Antoine was crazy. And what the hell was a guardian?

"Nessa," she heard her name being called from the front of the parlor. The voice sounded deep, guttural, familiar.

"Ailes!" she called back, and Antoine seemed to relax.

Ailes came into the room and stared at her before finally passing through the wall that she couldn't moments before. He gathered her into his arms and pulled her into a deep kiss.

Antoine cleared his throat. "We don't have time for this."

Ailes broke the kiss and looked at the guardian, nodding once. Then he looked down at Nessa and pushed a strand of free hair from her face. "You are going somewhere soon, and I can't accompany you." He smiled at her. "Anybody you meet and any choices you make, remember that I will be okay, and I won't be angry with you for choosing anything."

Nessa looked into Ailes' handsome face. He hadn't shaved in a while, and his clothes were wrinkled—uncharacteristic of the Ailes she had come to know and love. "You're scaring me. It's like you're trying to say good-bye."

When Ailes didn't say anything, Nessa pulled away from him, shaking her head. "Are you saying good-bye?"

Ailes still didn't answer

She walked to the chair and her tattoo gun. She laid her hand down on the chair, and that was when she noticed that she could see through her hand. She screamed.

Ailes pulled her into his arms once again as she yelled, "Why am I see-through? And how can you even touch me?"

"I am a half-demon, remember?"

~~*~*

Thirty minutes later, Ailes and Antoine had managed to calm the woman down.

Nessa was now staring at the chair, not speaking at all.

Antoine sighed and stopped picking at his fingernails. "Listen, you aren't dead. Just on the verge of dying."

Nessa looked at him. "Like I am near death? A near death experience?"

"Yes. Many people can go through it. You're only going through this because you're not like normal humans."

Ailes frowned at Antoine, who threw his hands in the air.

"Come on; she has to be told. I can't finish the job until she knows."

Nessa looked at both men. "Knows what?"

"Listen, you wanted to be the one to tell her, so now get on with it. Capisce?" Antoine told Ailes.

"Tell me what?" Nessa asked, looking at Ailes once more for answers.

Ailes rubbed his face then looked at Antoine, but the guardian refused to say anything else to help him. He sighed. "You're not human, Nessa. You never were."

Nessa walked around her old workroom at Hellish. *You're not human, Nessa. You never were.* How could that be? Her father wasn't different. He was human, wasn't he? What was she? Who was she?

"Please say something," Ailes asked for the third time.

"Yes, anything. A question. Something. Your pacing around is driving me nuts," Antoine said.

Nessa stopped and looked at them. "What do you want me to say? That I am not freaking out? Because I am. That I want to know more about you and myself? Because I do." She closed her eyes.

Antoine smiled. "I can answer some of your questions, but the others can only be answered by the relatives who await you beyond the wall. As for Ailes, I will let him tell you his dirty secrets. And I would be happy to tell you mine."

He chuckled. "I am Antoine, your guardian. I am here to help you through the wall so that you can make your choice to move on or stay here. That is my job." He looked at Ailes and pulled a bottle from his suit pocket, spun it on the ground, and forced it to face Ailes. "Your turn."

Ailes kicked the bottle away. "I am not a child anymore, Antoine, and this isn't Truth or Dare."

"Get it over with, Ailes," Nessa said, and Ailes looked at her.

"I met Billy when I was a teenager. I was a runaway and had nothing better to do than to believe that, because I was a half-demon, I was evil, or was supposed to be." Ailes smiled. "Your father believed I wasn't evil. He didn't know what I was, but he accepted me. It was Billy who found Isla for me when he searched for any relatives who might have been left from my mom's side and contacted her. Ellas couldn't help me because Lariat was out of control. After that, I just kept coming back to watch over him."

Nessa frowned. "So, you knew me then? Why didn't you say anything?"

"I knew what you looked like. I never met you in person. I was too busy with Isla and Lariat. And when I found out that Billy had a daughter who was near my age, I distanced myself as much as I could so Billy wouldn't get hurt. I knew then you were my mate, but I couldn't bring myself to meet you. I didn't want to believe it." Ailes winced. "He still wound up getting hurt eventually. His wife left him and you, and then he died because of me."

Nessa's lip trembled and tears spilled from her eyes. "It wasn't your fault … his death. If anything, it was mine. I was the one who provoked Mike."

Ailes looked at her. "No, Nessa, I shot him. I shot Billy, and now he is dead."

"What do you mean?"

"I shot him. I thought he was Mike, because Mike had changed his shape to look like Billy. I shot and didn't question it until I saw the tattoo that I had given Billy on his right hand. Mike could replicate that, and I hadn't known. I shot Billy, Nessa. I shot him." Ailes covered his face to hide the pain from her.

She didn't answer, and he thought that maybe she had just decided to leave him, but then warm arms embraced him. He brought his hands down to find Nessa hugging him.

"It's not your fault. It's Mike's. I'm not angry at you. How could I be? You saved me and Billy. You did what you could," Nessa whispered into his chest. "I forgive you, and Billy will, too. You still think you're not human?"

Ailes shook his head, and Nessa laid her head on his chest and closed her eyes, smiling when she heard his heartbeat. She then looked up at him with the most loving smile. "But your heart says otherwise, Ailes. The heart of a human who has seen too much pain."

Nessa looked at Antoine, and then the wall began to open up as if it were curtains. "I cannot stay here. I have to know what I am."

"I know. That's why I am not going to stop you, Nessa. I love you, and if that means I cannot be with you anymore, I can accept that," Ailes said.

Nessa smiled and pulled him in for a kiss. She caressed his unshaven cheek. "I will fight to come back to you. I may be angry when I do, because I'm sure that I will have some sort of slime on me when I come out of there."

Ailes laughed at the *Ghostbusters* pun.

"I will gladly take that anger and be willing to shower it off for you."

Nessa chuckled. "Then it's a date."

Nessa then looked at Antoine. "I am ready."

The guardian nodded and motioned for her to follow him toward the wall. Nessa smiled back at Ailes and Antoine.

Chapter 32

Nessa opened her eyes to find herself in a beautiful meadow, with flowers growing all around her. She was barefoot and wore a soft, pale blue dress.

She looked around as she walked. It was warm, unlike the cool air of Scotland, and not dreary as it had been before she had walked through the wall.

"Nessa," she heard Billy's voice call for her and ran toward it to find a young man walking toward her.

She hadn't seen him so young, not since she was nine.

"Daddy," she whispered as she ran into his arms. Arms that were still full of the vibrant tattoos that she had done for him when she had started out as an artist.

"I am so happy to see you, baby," he told her. "I am just sorry it has to be this way."

Nessa looked at him. "I am sorry you died. Ailes is beating himself up for killing you."

Billy smiled. "I'm not angry at Ailes for taking my life. Mike wasn't normal, and I assume he isn't dead either, because he isn't here. Ailes was fooled. He was a victim as much as I was. I knew that soon something like this might happen."

Nessa frowned. "What do you mean?"

"I was sick, Nessa. I had cancer and was in a lot of pain. It was only a matter of time before the radiation and chemo killed me," Billy explained.

When Nessa began to back away from him, he grabbed her arm and pulled her back. "Don't be angry with me. I couldn't tell you. Didn't know how."

Nessa pulled her arm away. "Just like you couldn't tell me that I'm not human?"

Billy's smile disappeared and sadness crept into his green eyes. "You were—are—my daughter. You always have been." He sighed. "I meant to tell you when your mother left, but you were so angry and upset that I didn't want to add to it. I promised that I would tell you when you were older, that I had plenty of time, but the years passed and soon you were a grown woman. Then Ailes came into the picture, and we were dealing with Mike stalking you." He shrugged. "I just couldn't do it. I didn't care who your parents were before you came to me. You are my daughter, and that's all that matters. I couldn't tell you that you were adopted."

"I was adopted?" Nessa frowned slightly. "Is that why Mom left me?"

"No, she left because she couldn't handle the thought of me being a tattoo artist. It's not a glamorous job that brings a decent paycheck. At least, back when I started it didn't. We struggled a lot."

"But didn't you want to know?" Nessa asked, changing the subject. "To look for my parents? To find out about me?"

"Sure, I did. Your mother even wanted to know." Billy winced. "I told her I would look into it but didn't for long. She left because she couldn't handle being a mother.

"I always wanted kids of my own but was unable to have them. You were my blessing, and I didn't want to give you back to people who might have abandoned you." Billy picked a pale-yellow flower and another quickly grew back in its place. He put it into her hair. "You were my sunshine. No grey skies from you. But then, you started to change.

"I noticed things that no human girl should be able to do. You healed faster than normal, and when you broke a bone, it was like you never broke it in the first place. Doctors were getting suspicious. That's when I knew I had to look into your birth. I had to know what I could be dealing with, so I contacted an old friend from my Army days and tasked him to find out as much as he could."

"Did he find anything?"

Billy shook his head. "Mikalio couldn't find anything. He tried, but the orphanage where I got you was gone, and no one remembered it had even existed."

"Mikalio is your friend?" Nessa asked in surprise.

"Yes. A strange demon he is. Not normal. Surprisingly nice and caring." Billy laughed. "What's wrong?"

"You knew Mikalio was a demon?"

"Well, sure, more so when I died than alive. But I guess, just like Ailes, I knew that, deep down, he was. I mean, during the war, he was able to do things that I couldn't. I didn't question it." Billy looked at the field beyond. "Mikalio was my friend. He saved my life countless times and helped me through my divorce from your mother. Who was I to judge?"

Nessa frowned. "But Mikalio told you he didn't find anything about the orphanage. And how did I not know about him?"

Billy shook his head. "If it existed at all, I'm sure he would have. But even your birth certificate was forged. Mikalio thought to leave it alone for my sake. You were living the life you were meant to … with me. Mikalio wasn't a part of our lives for long. He disappeared for a time."

He looked at her. "But remember, that is not why you are here. You are here because you have a choice to make. There is another here who wishes to speak with you. I don't know who she is, but she is very beautiful. She said she has been waiting for you since you visited her grave in Scotland."

"I thought I was supposed to talk to my relatives, like Grandpa and Grandma or something like that?"

"I ran away from home, and even then, it was a foster home. I didn't know my mom and dad, which is probably one of my biggest reasons for adopting you."

Billy nodded toward a large tree in the field. "You need to speak with her. She has something to tell you, something important. For Ailes, I wouldn't keep her waiting."

Nessa looked at the tree then at Billy again. "I don't want to leave you yet. I have so many questions for you, and I don't understand why I can't stay."

Billy's smile went away, and she could feel his sadness. He nudged her toward the tree, but Nessa floated back. "Go talk to her. You will always have me. I am your father. I just want you to know you have more to accomplish. Go and don't look back." He blew her a kiss. "I love you, baby," he told her then disappeared.

"No, Daddy! Wait! I need you. Please don't go," Nessa cried, running to the spot where he had been, but before she made it there, she found herself by the big tree and staring into the face of a brown-haired beauty.

"Hello, Nessa," the woman said, motioning her to sit next to her by the tree. "Come talk to me a while."

Nessa looked back up the hill where her dad had been then sat down next to the woman.

The woman smiled and smoothed out her pale pink dress. "It's beautiful here, isn't it?"

"Yeah, and warmer than Scotland." Nessa snorted, and the woman laughed.

"It's been a long time since I felt the cold air of Scotland," the woman said. "I loved the snow and the cool breeze."

"Why are you here?" Nessa asked. "Who are you?"

The woman looked at her. "I am Nyla. My mother is Isla, and Ailes is my son."

"You're Ailes' mother?"

"I am." Nyla laughed. "I am also one of the guardians who look after those who will pass on to the next life."

"Like Antoine."

"Yes, like Antoine," Nyla said. "The only difference is that Antoine is in the living world, and I am part of the death division. Two separate divisions, and sometimes we don't mingle, but I took a special interest in you when you visited my grave." She smiled. "You are in love with my son, after all, so how could I not take on your case?"

"I can leave?" Nessa asked.

"Your choice. Billy has already appealed for you, though you're needed in the living world more than here in the dead one. And my son needs to know who my killers were, and you need to know who you were meant to be before Billy adopted you." Nyla sighed. "That's going to be harder than you think."

"Because the orphanage I came from no longer exists or never did?"

"That, and whoever put you up for adoption simply didn't want anyone to know who you belonged to. Unfortunately, the guardian department cannot help with that. Other departments can. Maybe the Nightingales will know. But they are crabby at best, just like the FBI in the States. But, if you can find someone to help you from that organization, then you might have more luck," Nyla explained.

Nessa nodded. "And that's why I can't stay. It's not that my dad vouched for me, but because I can't leave yet. I want to be with your son, have a family. I am not ready to leave yet."

"Sounds like a good choice. Remember, though, you are always wanted on our end, but when it's too soon, we can't really move you here. Too much paperwork," Nyla explained.

"Fine, I guess that means I need to know who killed you, and then go back home for my date. I did promise Ailes, after all," Nessa said.

Nyla laughed. "Good to hear." She stood. "As for who killed me, I didn't know who sent those demons after me, but I have a suspicion. I believed it must have been Lariat at first, but he barely even looked at me, and the only time he touched me was during sex. I don't know for sure who sent them. I do know they were agents. Federal agents. I don't know if DPAI is connected to this."

"So, I am supposed to find this person?" Nessa asked.

Nyla shook her head again. "No, Brylan is. He is a part of the Nightingales. It's his job but telling my son can bring him closure so he stops acting like an arse and blaming himself. It would help my heart, too.

"I'm sorry that I'm asking you to do this for me, since it's against regulations."

"Don't apologize. I will help you as much as I can, regulations or not," Nessa promised. "Now, can I leave?"

"Oh, I almost forgot." Nyla parted the wall as Antoine did before. "It may take some time before you wake up, so while you wait, please remember this: Things aren't always what they appear to be and never judge a book by its cover." She laughed. "God, it's been so long since I felt like a mom. Now get your ass to your date."

Chapter 33

$\mathbf{A}$iles watched as Isla and Ellas fussed over Nessa as they waited for her to come back to them. The guardians had a long process when one was near death, and the doctor and nurse had to ensure enough oxygen got to Nessa's brain to determine that she would make it in life. He wasn't worried. He knew Antoine would get her through.

Nessa woke slowly, and everyone was relieved that she had made it through the coma.

Mikalio walked over to the women then led them out of the room to give the couple some much needed space. He never thought he would see this day. It definitely wouldn't have happened with Lariat around.

He was still shocked that he had another son—Nyla having kept Ailes a secret from him for so long. He had always thought Lariat had fathered Ailes, but after the crowning, he had known the boy was his. A simple paternity spell proved that to be correct, as Ailes could only be an elder if he had the bloodline to take the clan's mantle. He had wanted to know for so long since Lariat seemed to have been sterile. Therefore, it was only natural that he had fathered Ailes and Ellas.

Mikalio watched Nyla kiss their son's forehead.

Only he could see her. But that was Nyla. She didn't want to be seen but allowed herself only to Mikalio.

Then Nyla floated out to the balcony of the room, and Mikalio followed her.

"He has your eyes," he told her. "Just like his grandmother."

Nyla looked at him. "He has more of you in him than me."

"More Isla, but a little of me and you."

Nyla chuckled. "You know that's what I miss about you, Mikalio—your inability to decide how handsome you are."

"Why did you leave, Nyla?"

Nyla looked out onto the garden below them. "I had to protect Ailes from Lariat, but I failed, and he still got to him. I was going to tell you, but I hadn't the heart."

"You have been around me for so long now, since the day you died and came back from the city of the dead, so why didn't you tell me I fathered Ailes in the first place? Why did I have to cast a spell to find out?" he asked.

"This is not the time to talk about this, my love. Go see our soon-to-be daughter-in-law. Soon, there will be a new birth."

"No, it *is* the right time! Dammit, Nyla! What do you mean a new birth?" Mikalio asked, but Nyla had disappeared.

Brylan and Ellas walked onto the balcony.

"Nessa and Ailes want to speak with you," Ellas told Mikalio.

Chapter 34

9 Months Later…

Ailes walked Evangeline down the aisle toward her mother and the love of his life.

Nessa smiled and, just as Evangeline made it to her, she scooped her into her arms and gave her a big ol' kiss. Evangeline laughed.

Mikalio began the ceremony that finished just as fast as it had started.

Nessa was surprised and happy to see Meagan, who sat in a wheelchair that Samuel pushed toward her and Ailes.

"She is so beautiful!" Meagan said, playing with Evangeline's tiny hand.

"Would you like to hold her?" Nessa asked.

"Can I?" Meagan looked at her dad, and when he nodded, Nessa put Evangeline in Meagan's lap. "Oh, I just love babies."

Evangeline leaned into Meagan's chest and settled in. Her expression told her parents that she was at peace.

"We have to go talk to our guests. Do you think you can handle her?" Nessa asked.

"Oh, sure, I am the baby whisperer." Meagan looked at her dad. "You can go, too. I have this handled."

They left Evangeline with Meagan, but Nessa looked back and was shocked to see that Evangeline had fallen asleep in Meagan's arms. She immediately felt much better about leaving her with the woman.

~~*~*

Meagan stroked the girl's short, black hair then her chubby cheeks. She loved babies so much and wished she could have one of her own. Just like Evangeline.

"On baby duty?" she heard Brylan's deep, guttural voice as he came to sit in a chair next her.

"Better than being out there. At least I have a chair already. Don't have to fight them with the baby either."

"A baby in your arms suits you," Brylan said.

Meagan frowned. "Are you flirting with me?"

Brylan laughed. "Is that what I'm doing?"

Meagan snorted, maneuvering Evangeline before she began to wheel away from Brylan. However, the infuriating man just scooped up the baby and pushed her along.

"Where would you like to go?" he asked.

Meagan pushed down the stoppers. "Nowhere. Just trying to get away from you."

Brylan laughed. "Yeah, but you aren't taking the baby with you. You can hardly wheel away."

Meagan shook her head and unstopped the wheels before wheeling away from Brylan.

"Some woman, isn't she?" he asked a sleeping Evangeline.

~~*~*

Mike watched the woman wheel away from the half-fae and smiled. If he couldn't have Nessa, then he would have Meagan. What a sweet name. It rolled off his tongue in a pleasant sound.

He would have her start his new harem, and then he would hunt down the child and take her from Nessa and Ailes. They would pay for wounding him.

"Brother," he heard Lariska say from behind him.

Mike turned and found her almost nose to nose with him.

171

She hissed and grabbed him around his neck.

"Throw him into the dungeons," he heard Elder Kainez's raspy voice from behind her.

Mike felt his human form tremble, and soon, he was in his original form. His horns burst forth from his skull, and his eye throbbed with pain as the mortal coil left. He tried to use whatever magic he could to break free, but Lariska's grasp was too strong, centuries of power in a tight, compact body. He knew then that pleading, changing their minds, and begging for forgiveness wasn't an option. He would die there in that dungeon, and Lenarska would see to that.

"It would be my pleasure," Lariska said as she smiled.

FIN

About the Author

T.M. Dawson is voracious reader, who enjoys crafts, spending time with family, drawing, and writing Paranormal Romance. She is a Texas native, living with her husband, black dog, and cat.

You can find her on:

Facebook Author Page:
https://www.facebook.com/AuthorT.M.Dawson/?ref=bookmarks

Facebook Group:
https://www.facebook.com/groups/496043341233035/

Pinterest:
https://www.pinterest.com/Tmdawson09/

Blog:
https://authortmdawson.blogspot.com

Website:
https://tmdawson0.wixsite.com/website

www.ingramcontent.com/pod-product-compliance
Lightning Source LLC
Chambersburg PA
CBHW020333110726
47898CB00003B/852